To Mati and Marce

Syncretic Press

Published by Syncretic Press, LLC.
PO Box 7401, Wilmington, Delaware 19803
www.syncreticpress.com
Direct all questions to info@syncreticpress.com

©2021 by Syncretic Press, LLC — First edition in English
Between the lines, by Marcos Severi
Text and illustrations by Marcos Severi
Translation by Karen Schleeweis
Translation contributor: Charlotte Whittle.
Author's picture by Gaby Leigue
ISBN: 978-1-946071-29-3
Library of Congress Control Number: 2020934561

Most of the content on Between the lines comes from the book Severi en línea (in Spanish).
First published in Argentina © 2018 by Del Naranjo S.R.L.
ISBN 978-987-3854-49-1. Available in the U.S. at www.syncreticpress.com
Text and illustrations copyright © 2018 by Marcos Severi
Facebook: @marcos.severi - Instagram: @severimarcos
www.mseveri.com

Printed in China

Severi
BETWEEN THE LINES

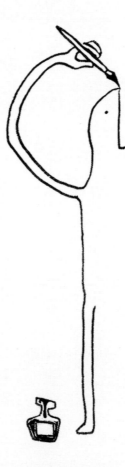

Syncretic Press

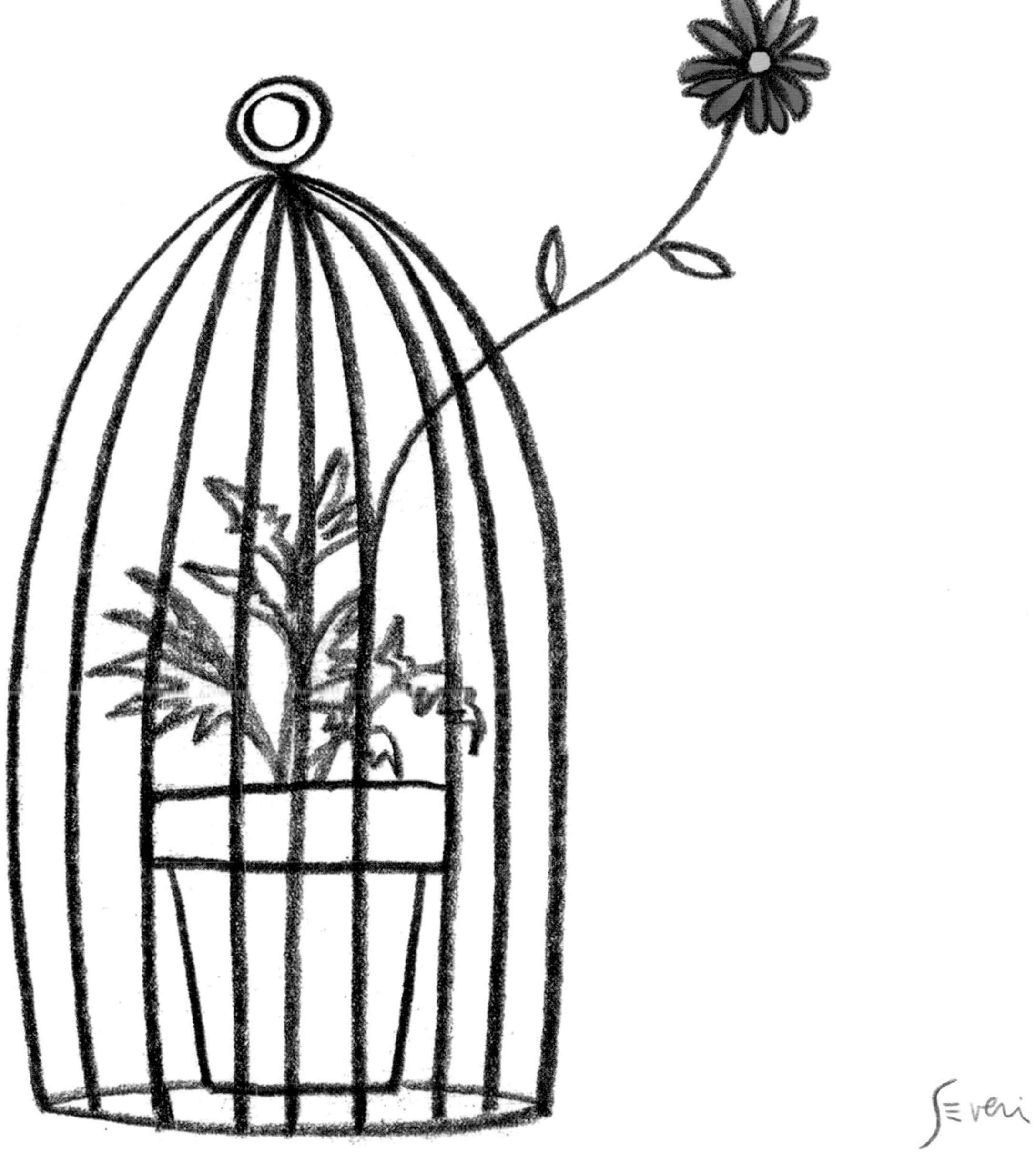
Severi

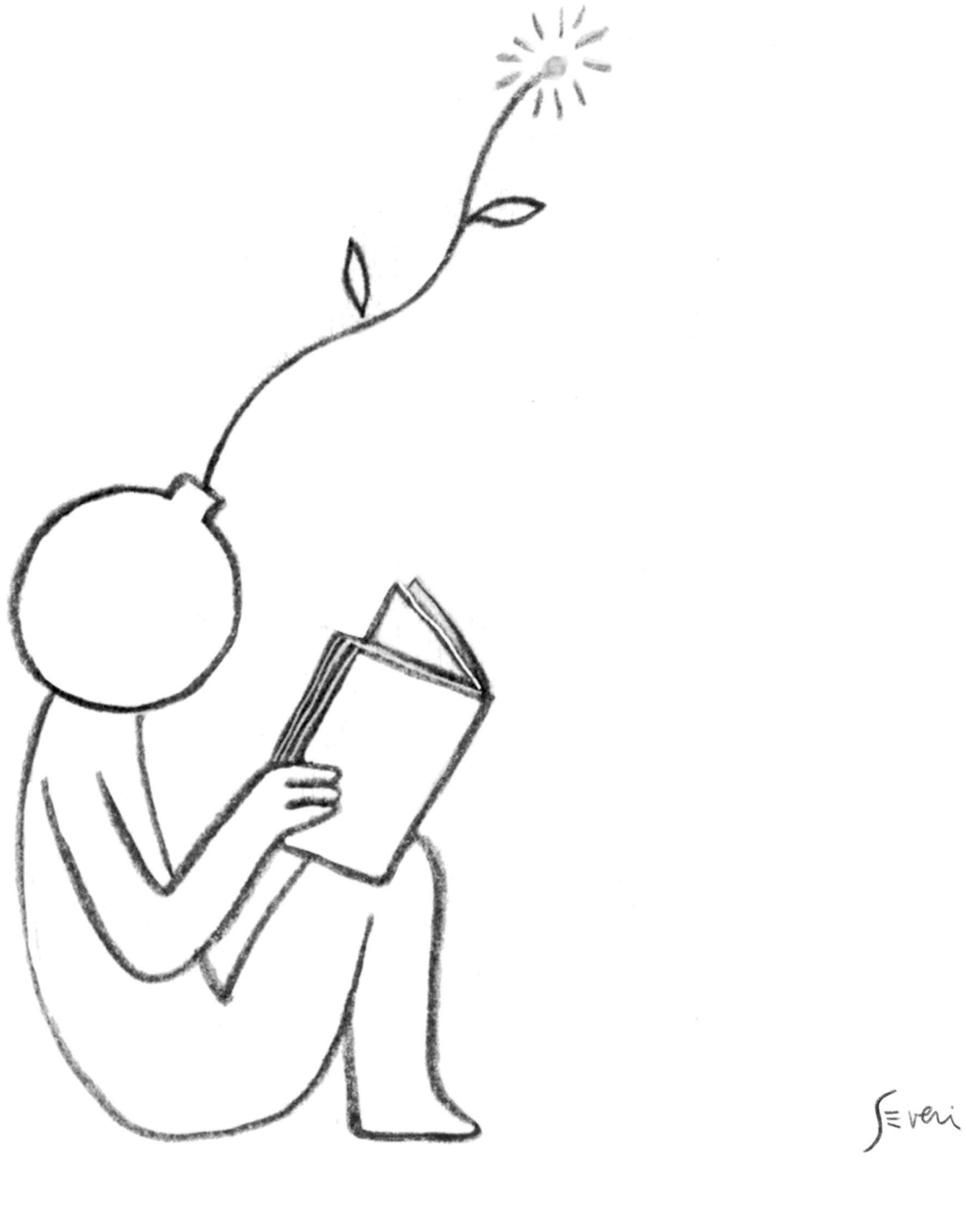
Severi

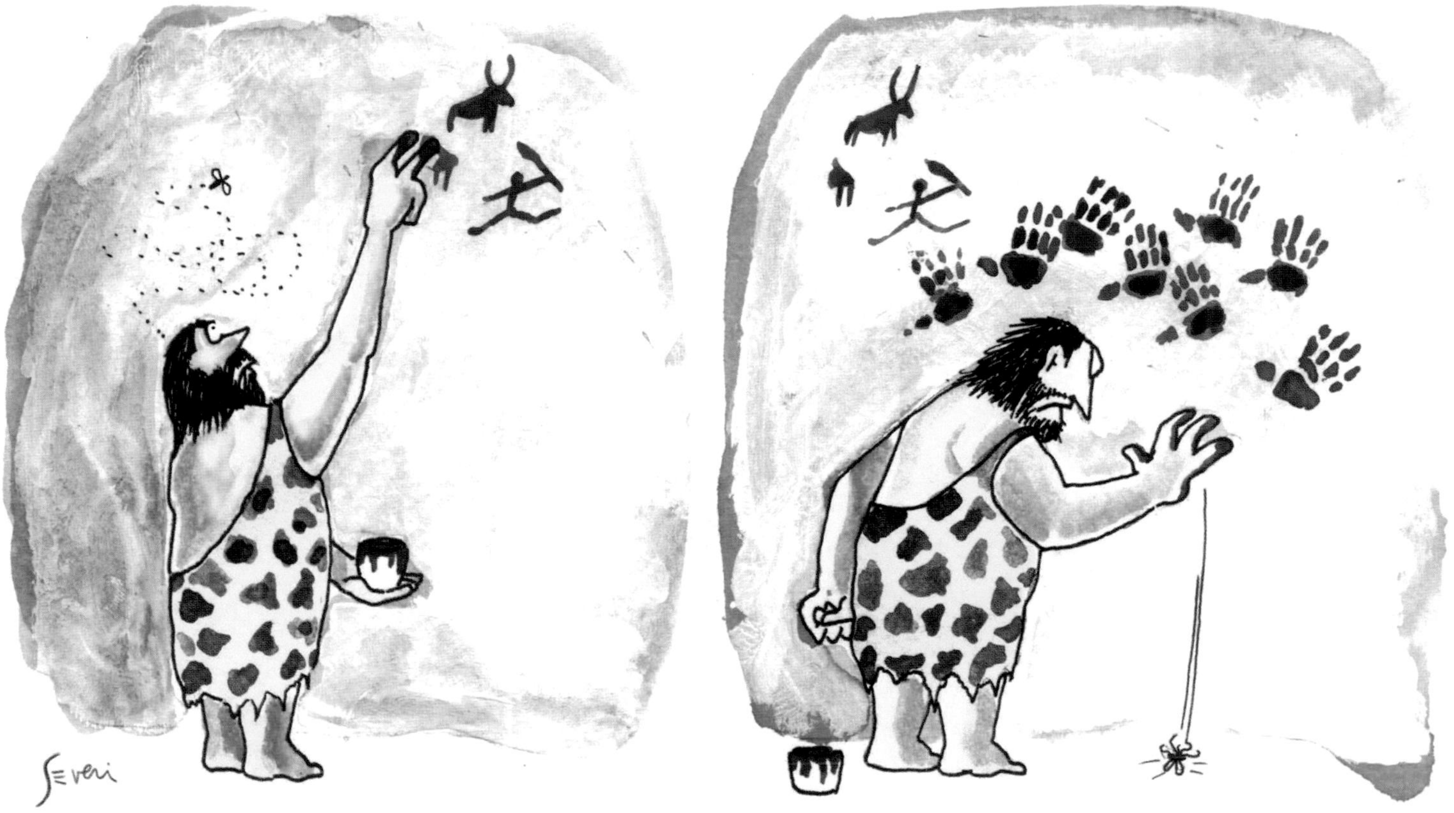
Severi

YOUR ROOTS ARE INTACT, YOU'LL FLOWER AGAIN.

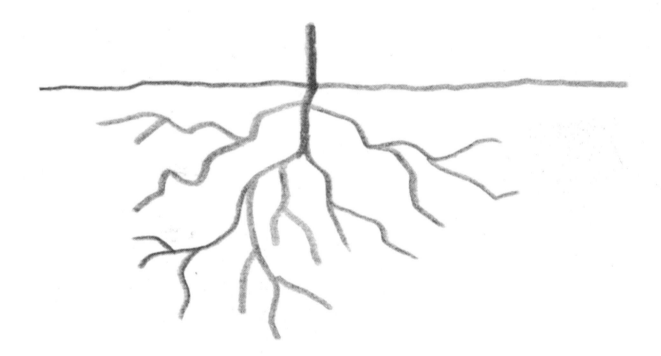

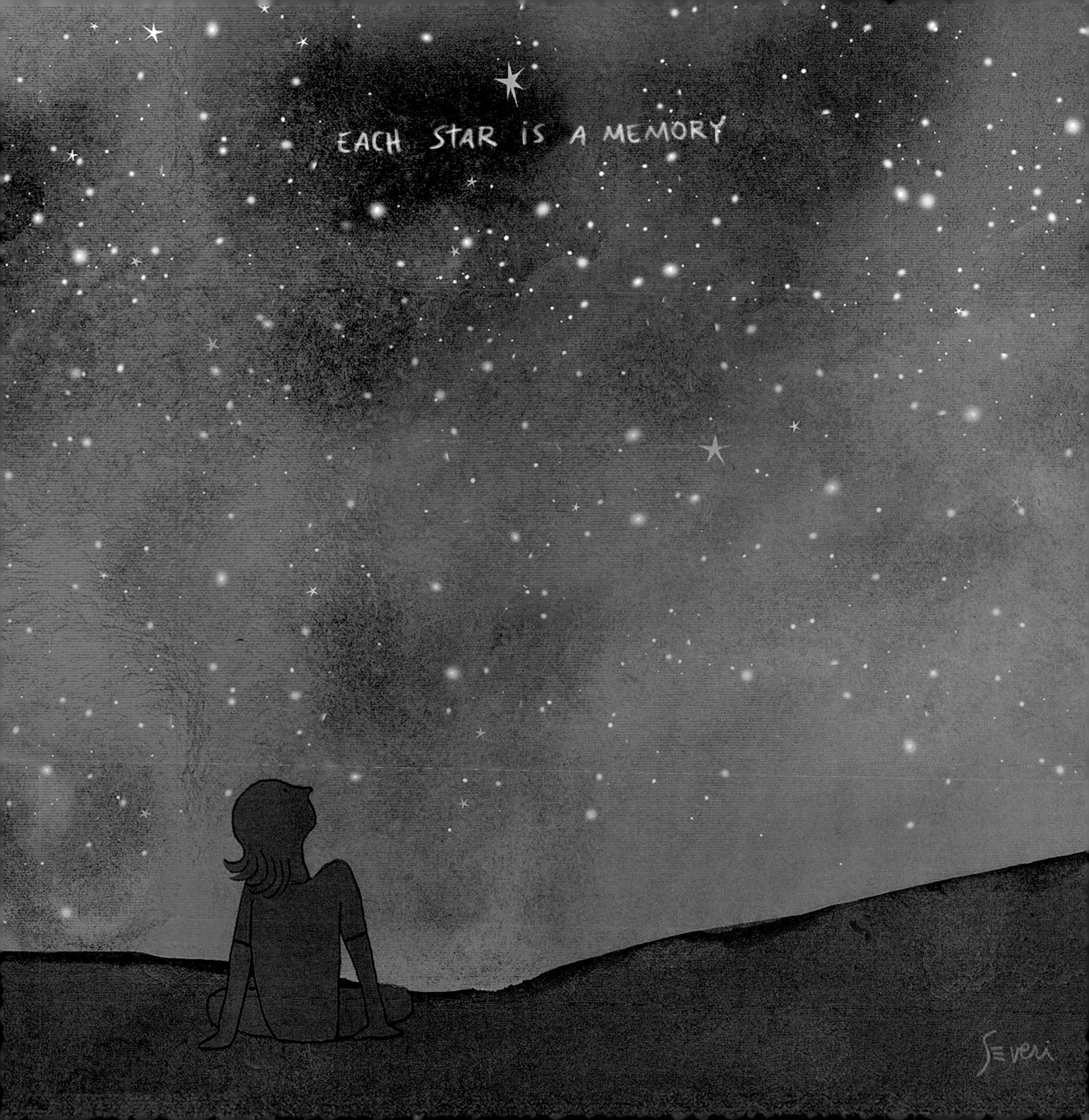
EACH STAR IS A MEMORY
Severi

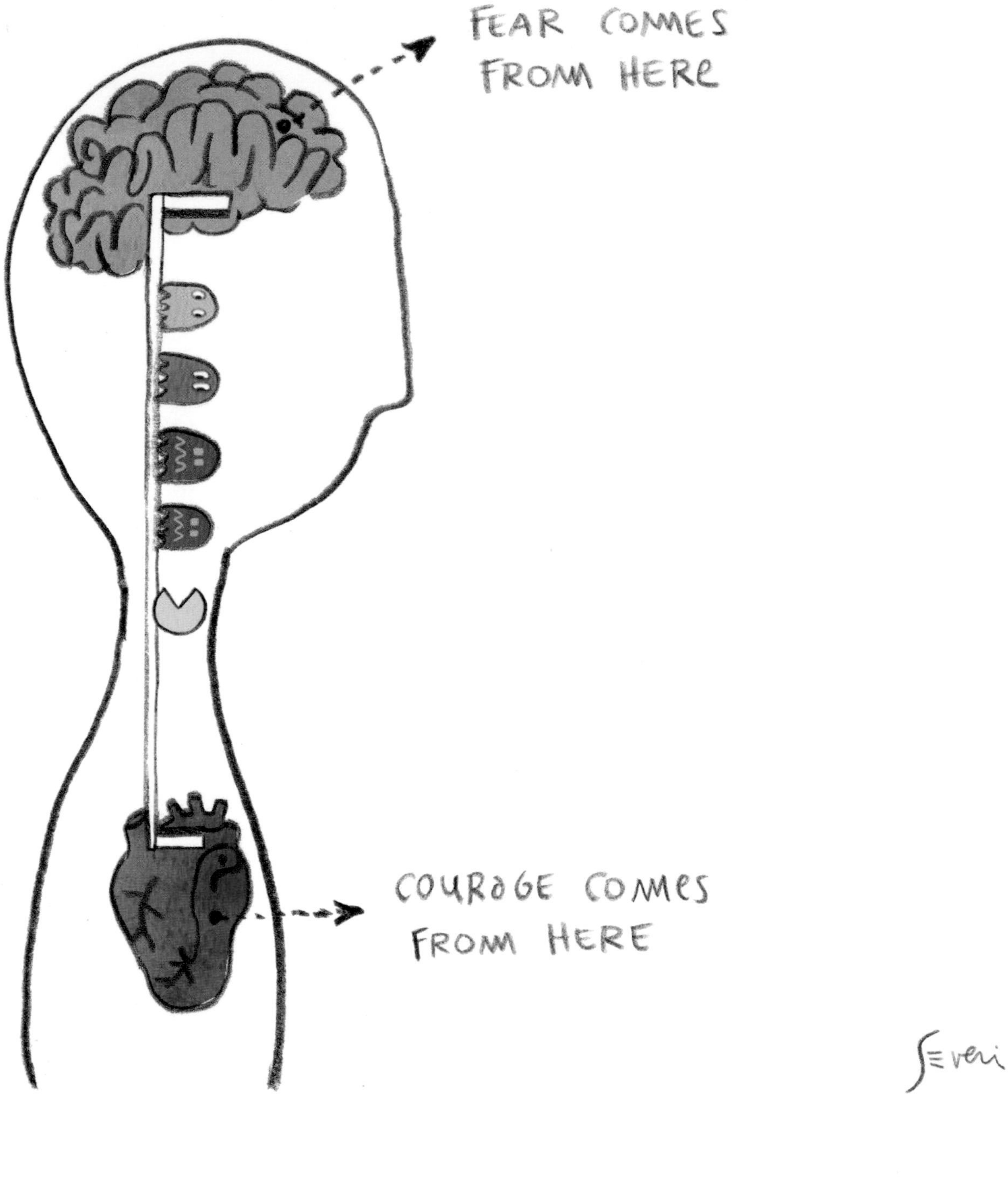
FEAR COMES FROM HERE
COURAGE COMES FROM HERE
Severi

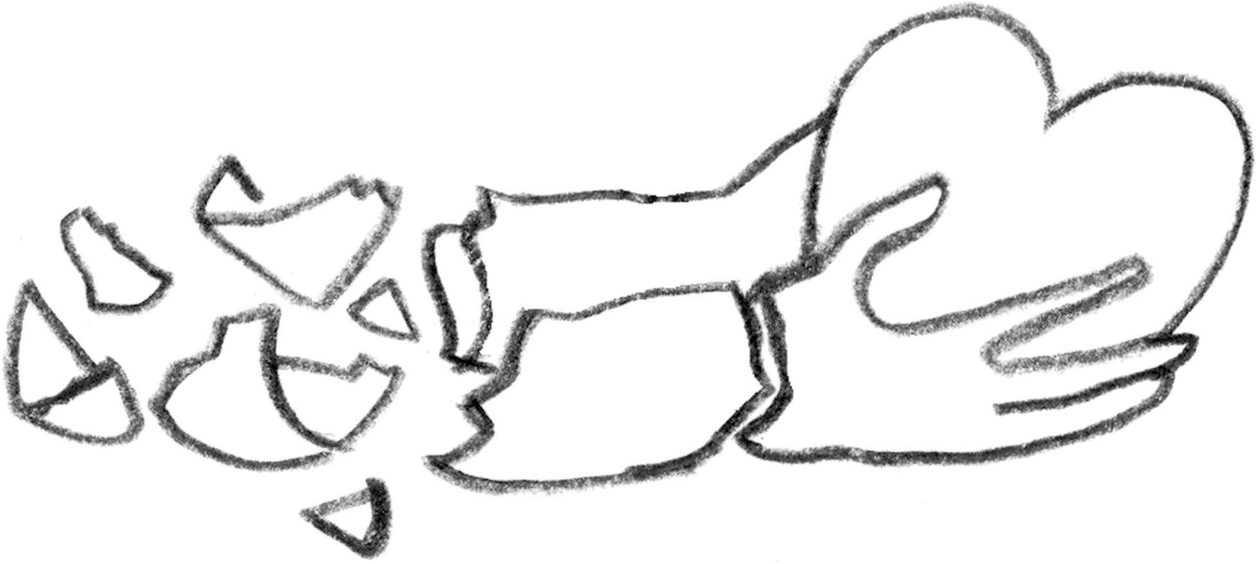

Severi

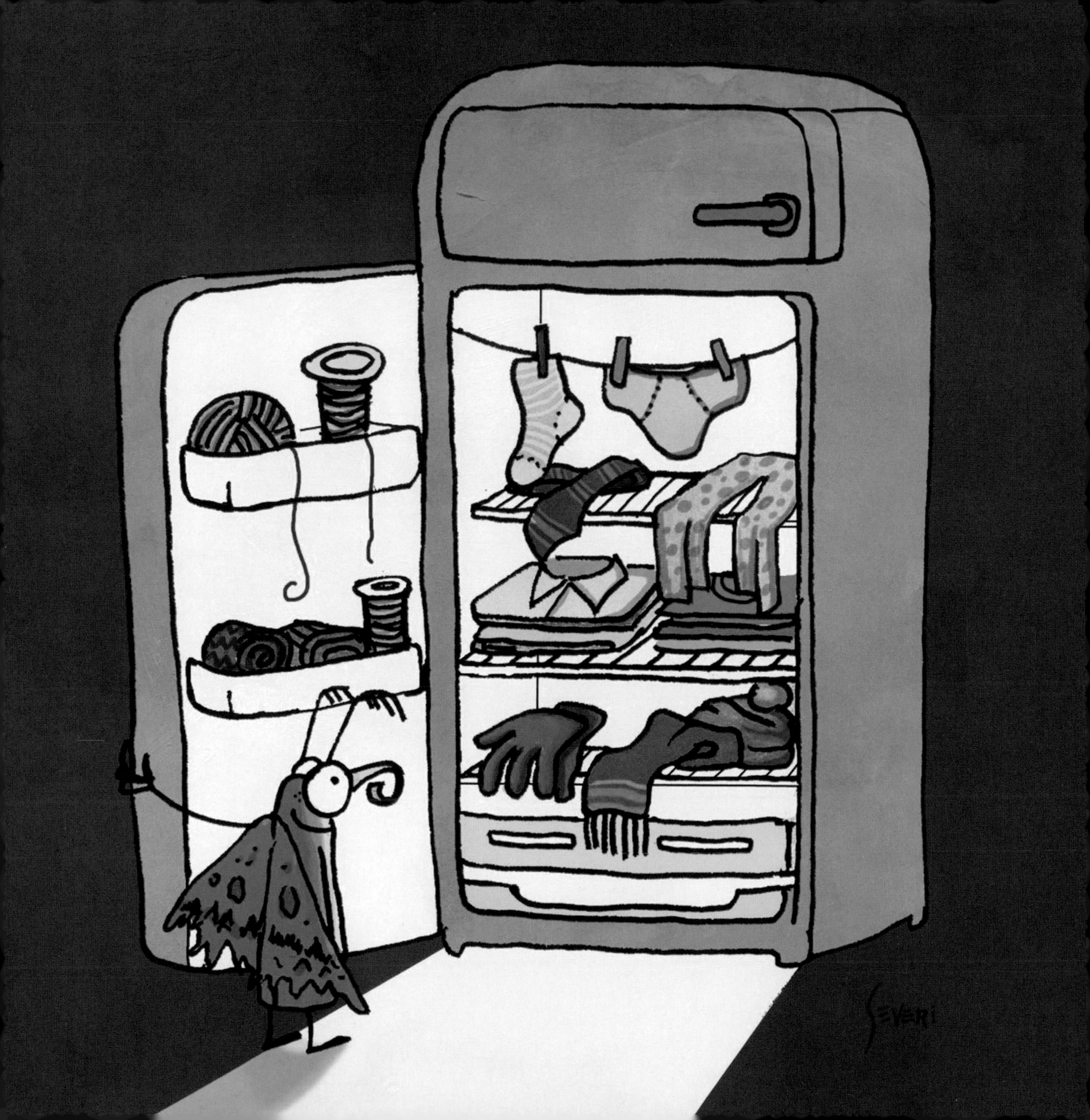
SEVERI

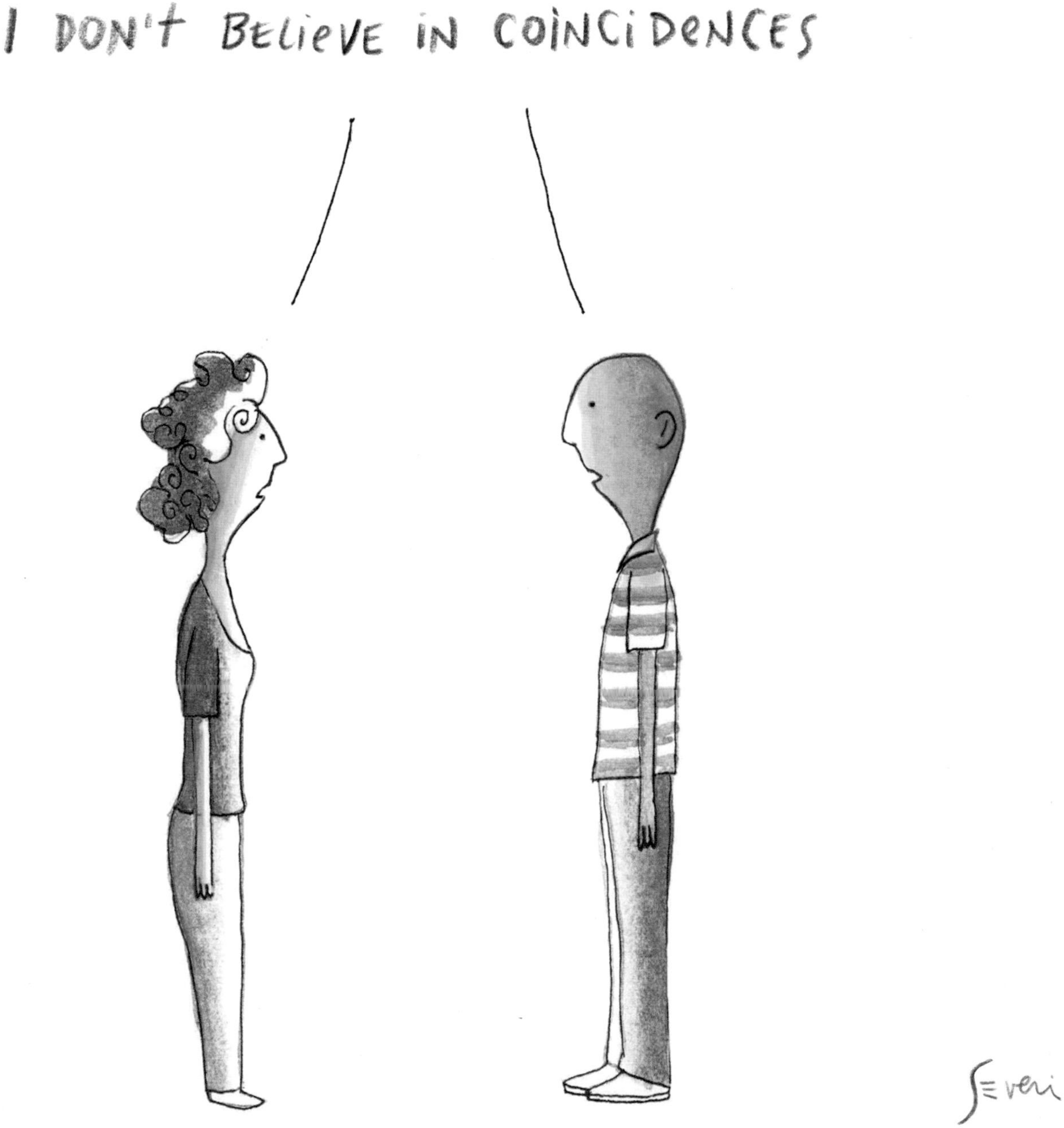
I DON'T BELIEVE IN COINCIDENCES
Severi

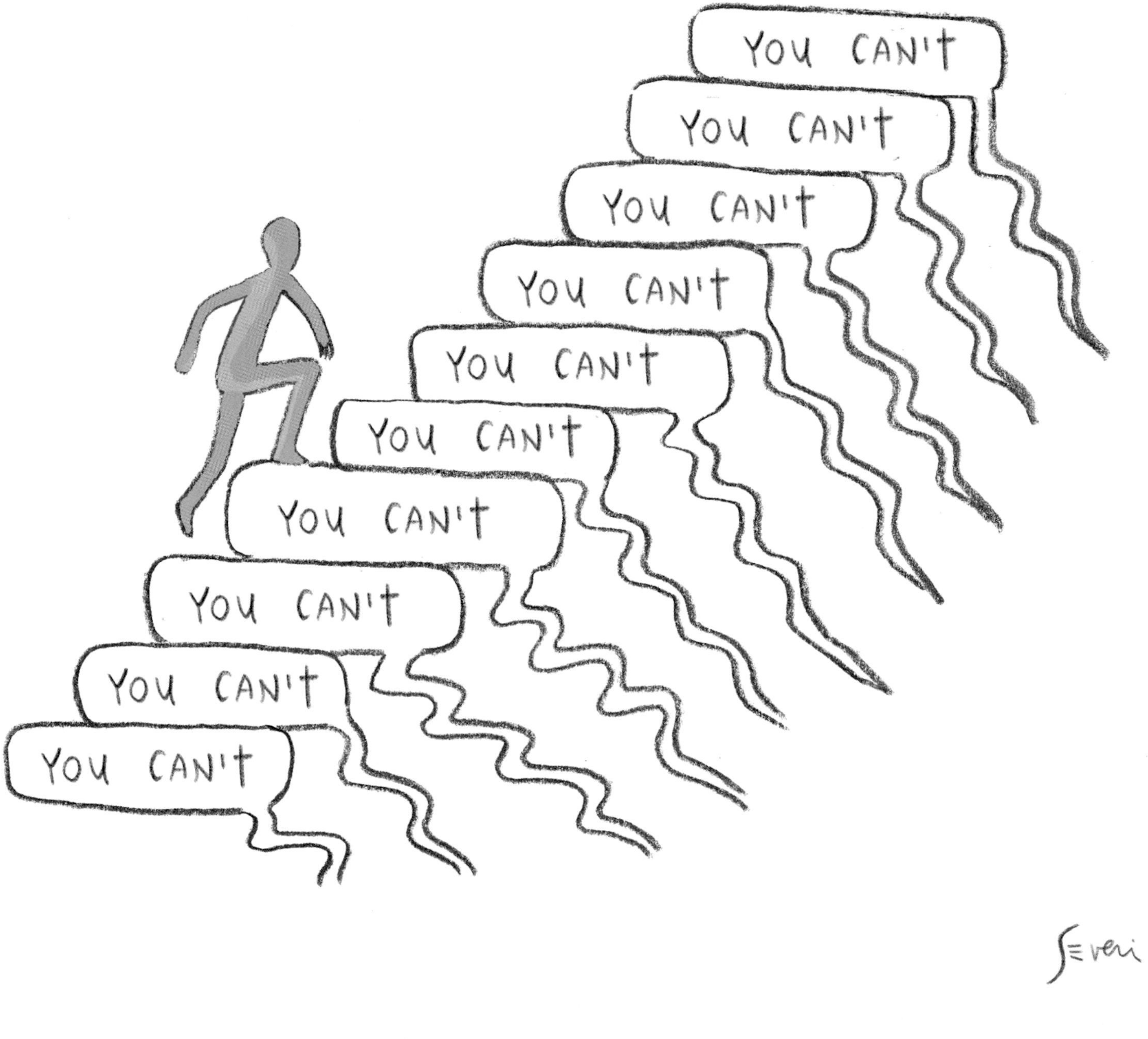
YOU CAN'T
YOU CAN'T
YOU CAN'T
YOU CAN'T
YOU CAN'T
YOU CAN'T
YOU CAN'T
YOU CAN'T
YOU CAN'T
YOU CAN'T
Severi

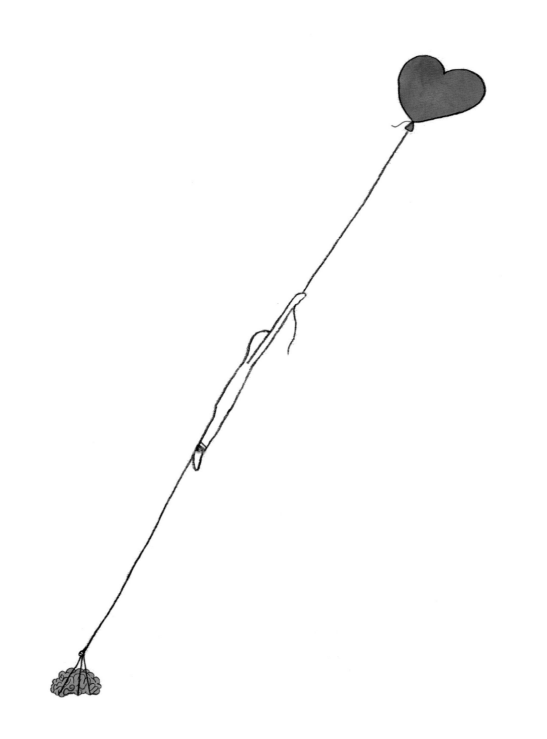

HOW DOES SHE KNOW I AM CRYING?

Severi

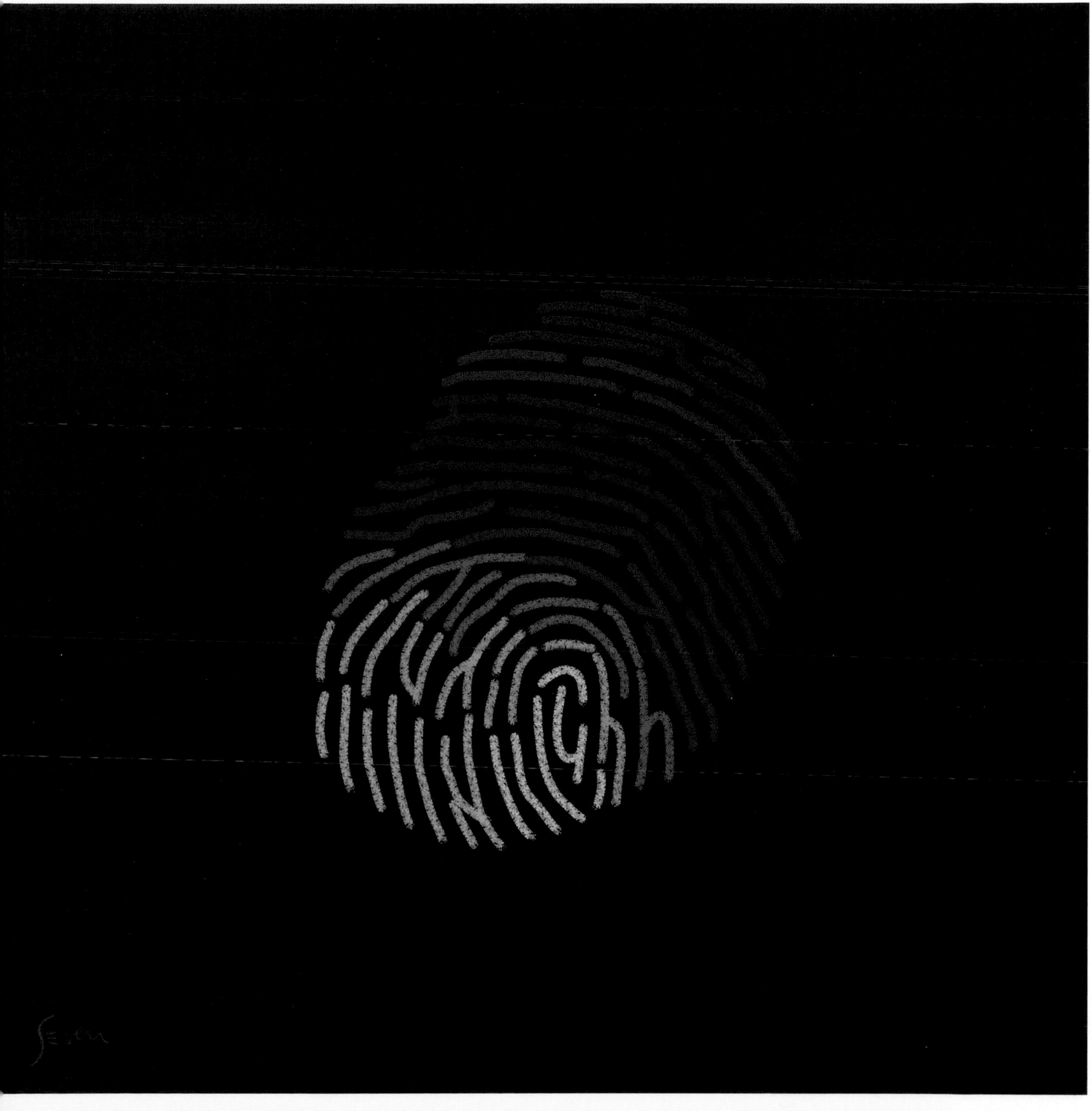

THE SEA SEPARATES THEM...

OR CONNECTS THEM?

Severi

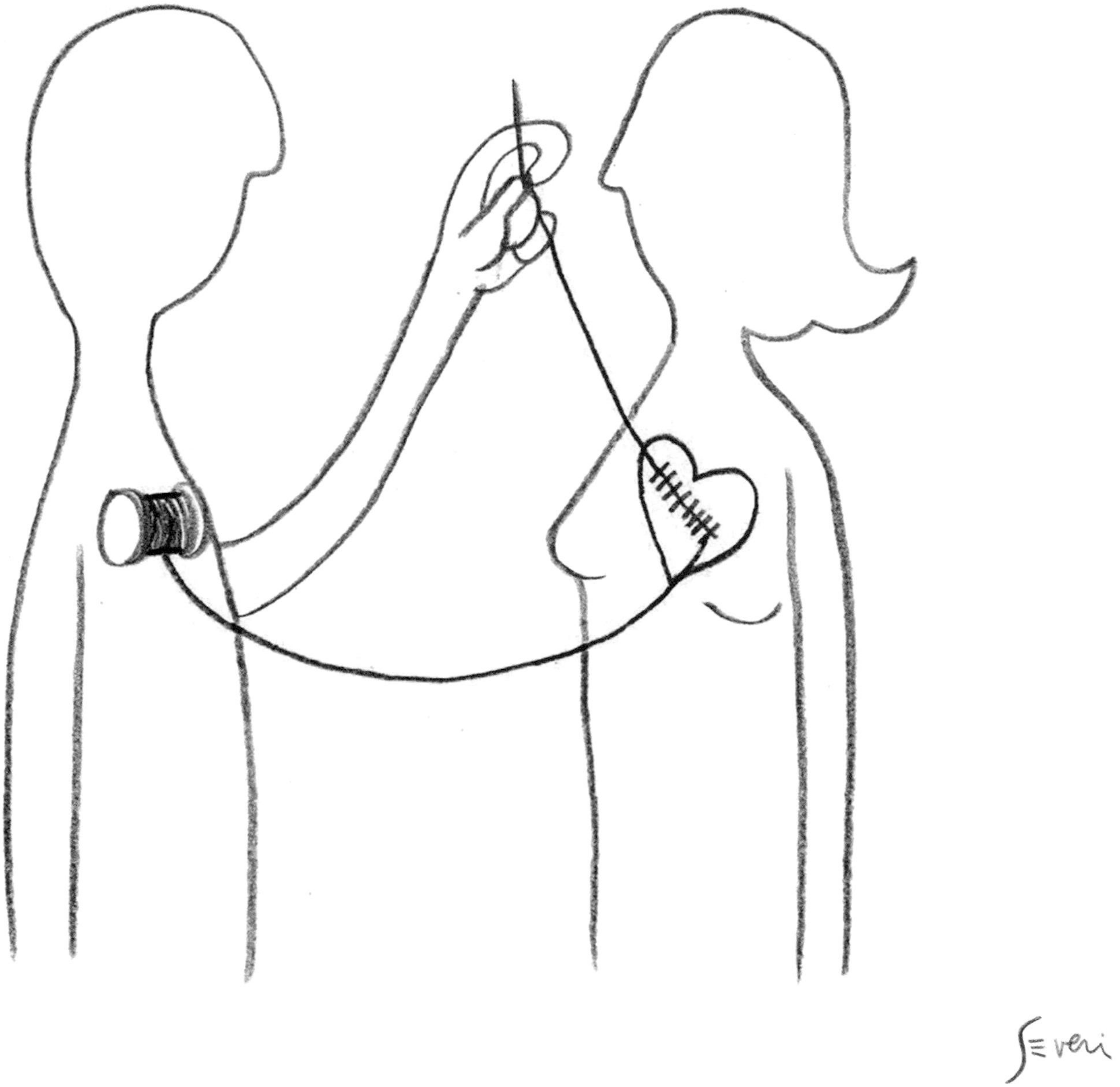
Severi

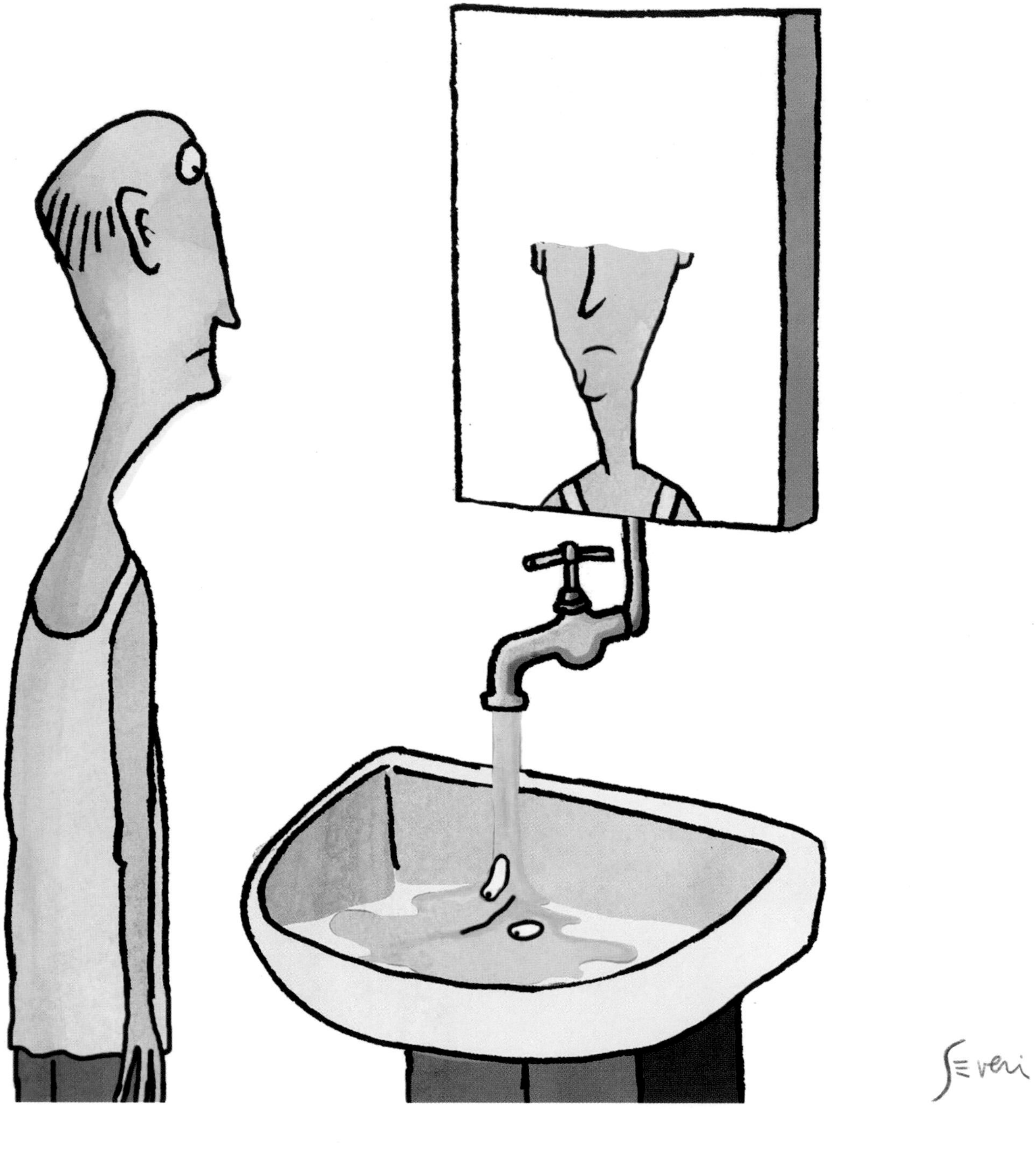
Severi

HE FELL IN LOVE YESTERDAY...
BUT IS NOT AWARE YET.

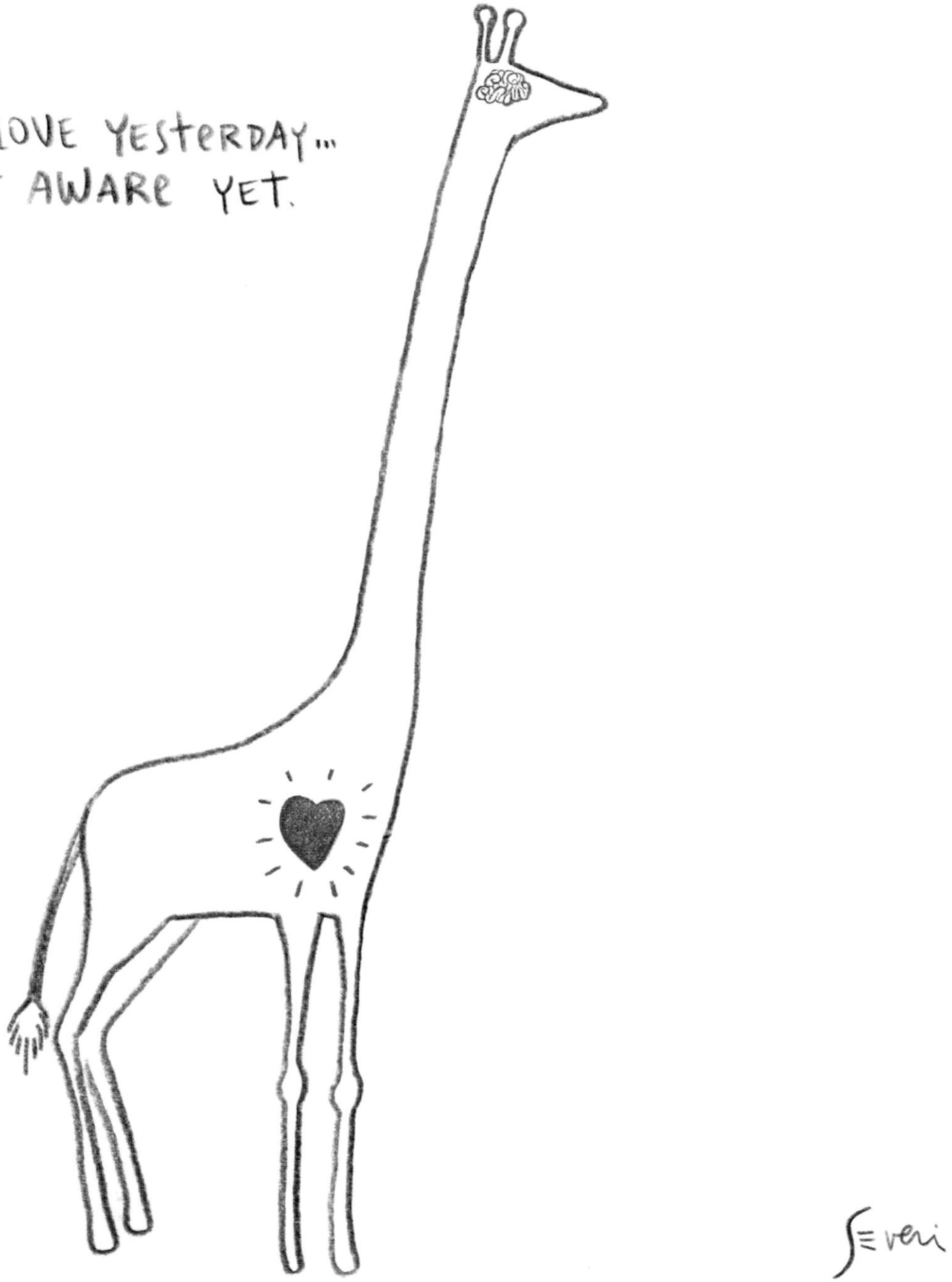
Severi

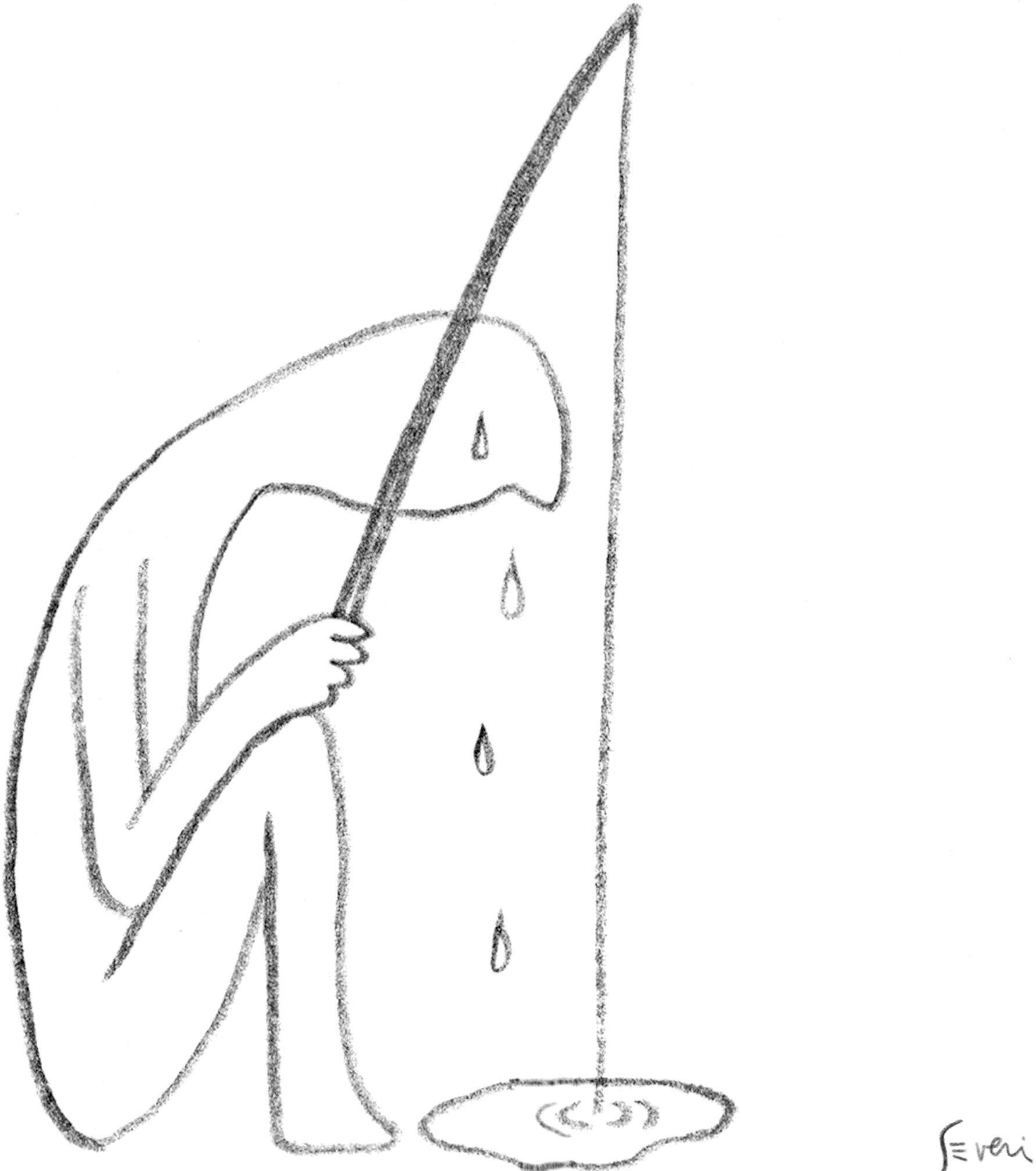
Severi

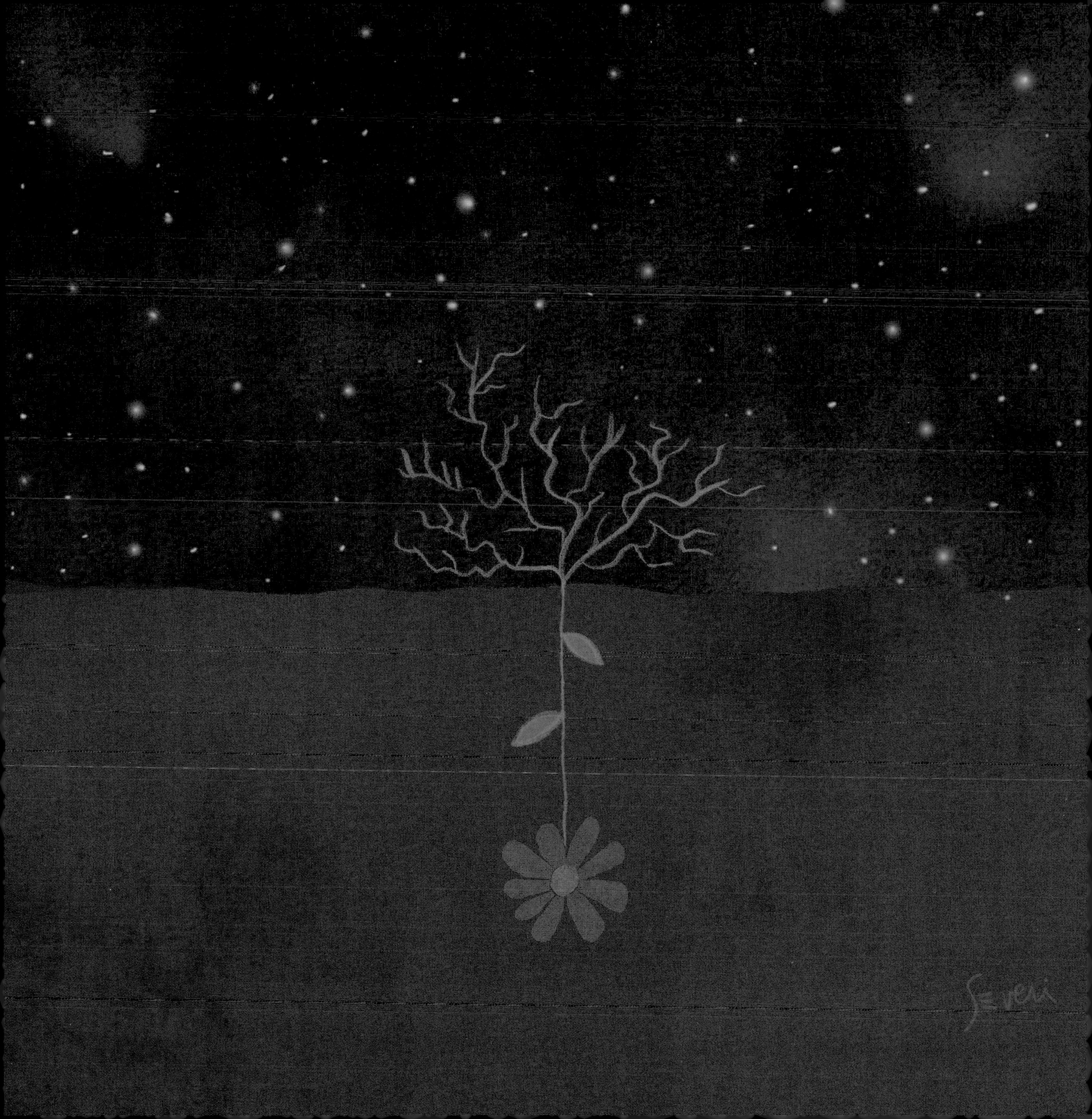
Severi

simplicity is bliss

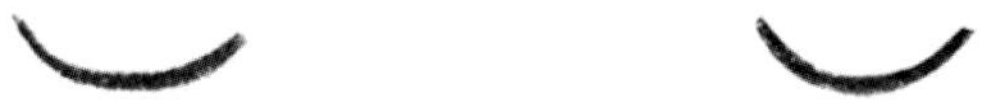

Severi

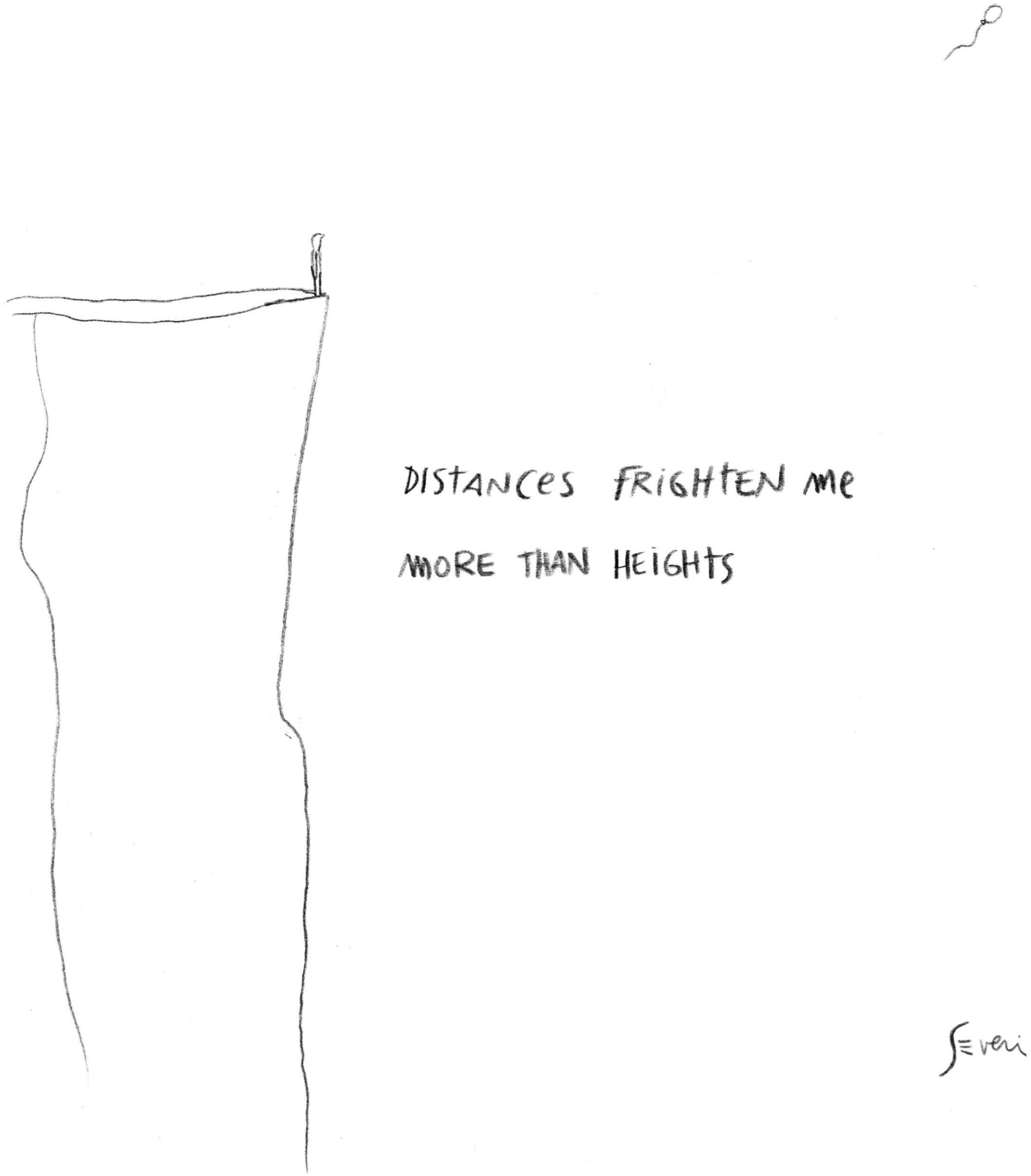
DISTANCES FRIGHTEN ME
MORE THAN HEIGHTS
Severi

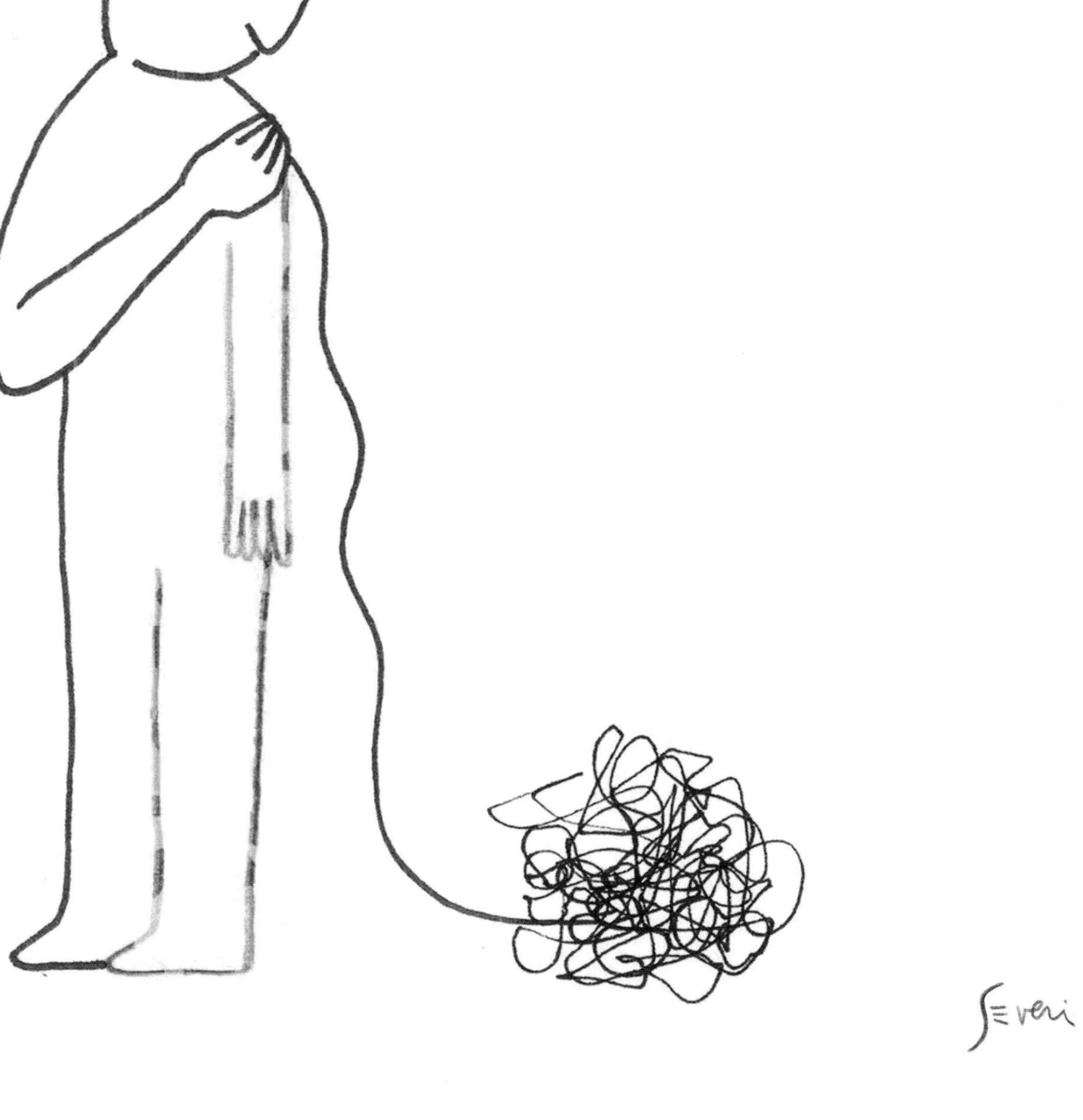
Severi

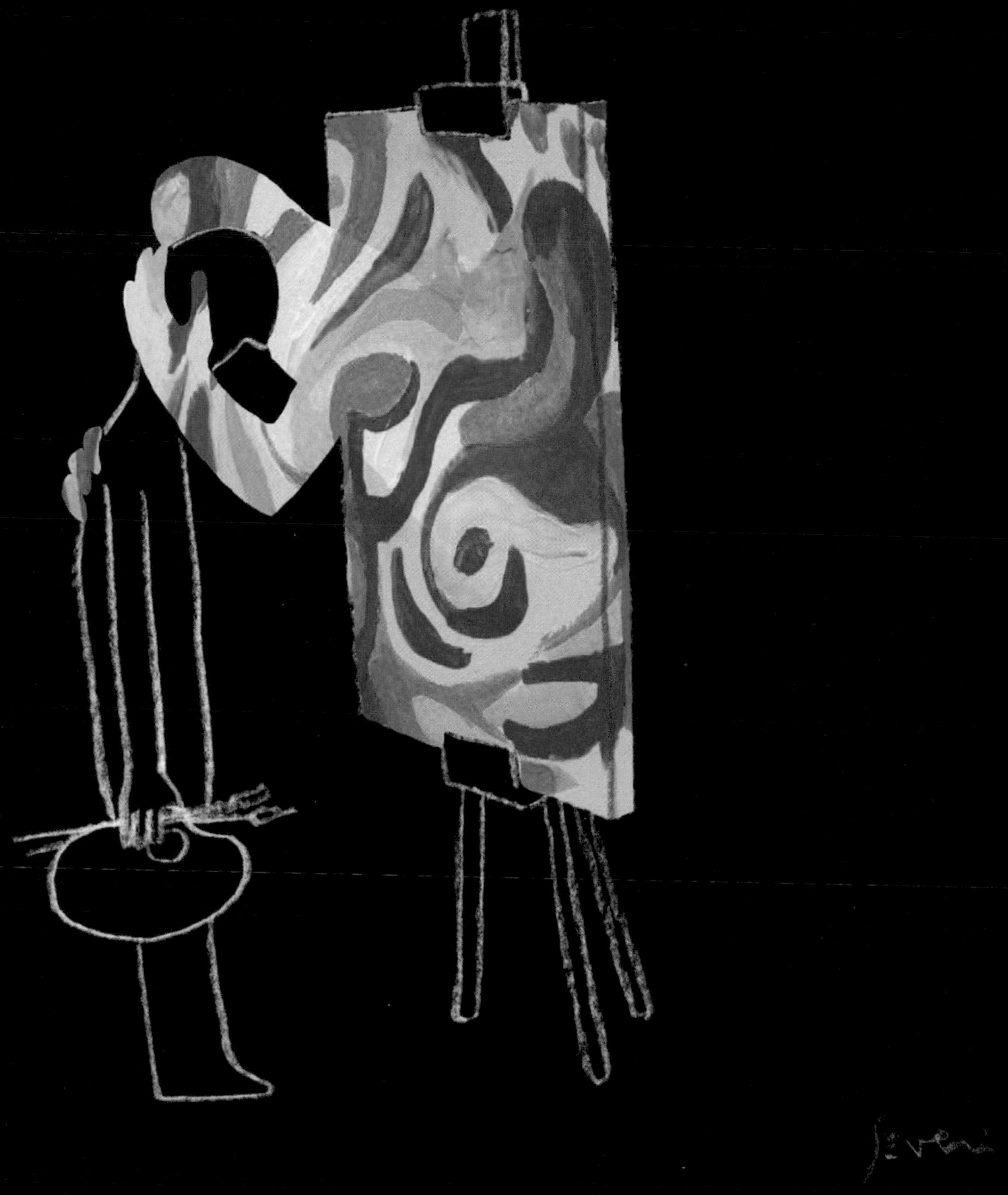

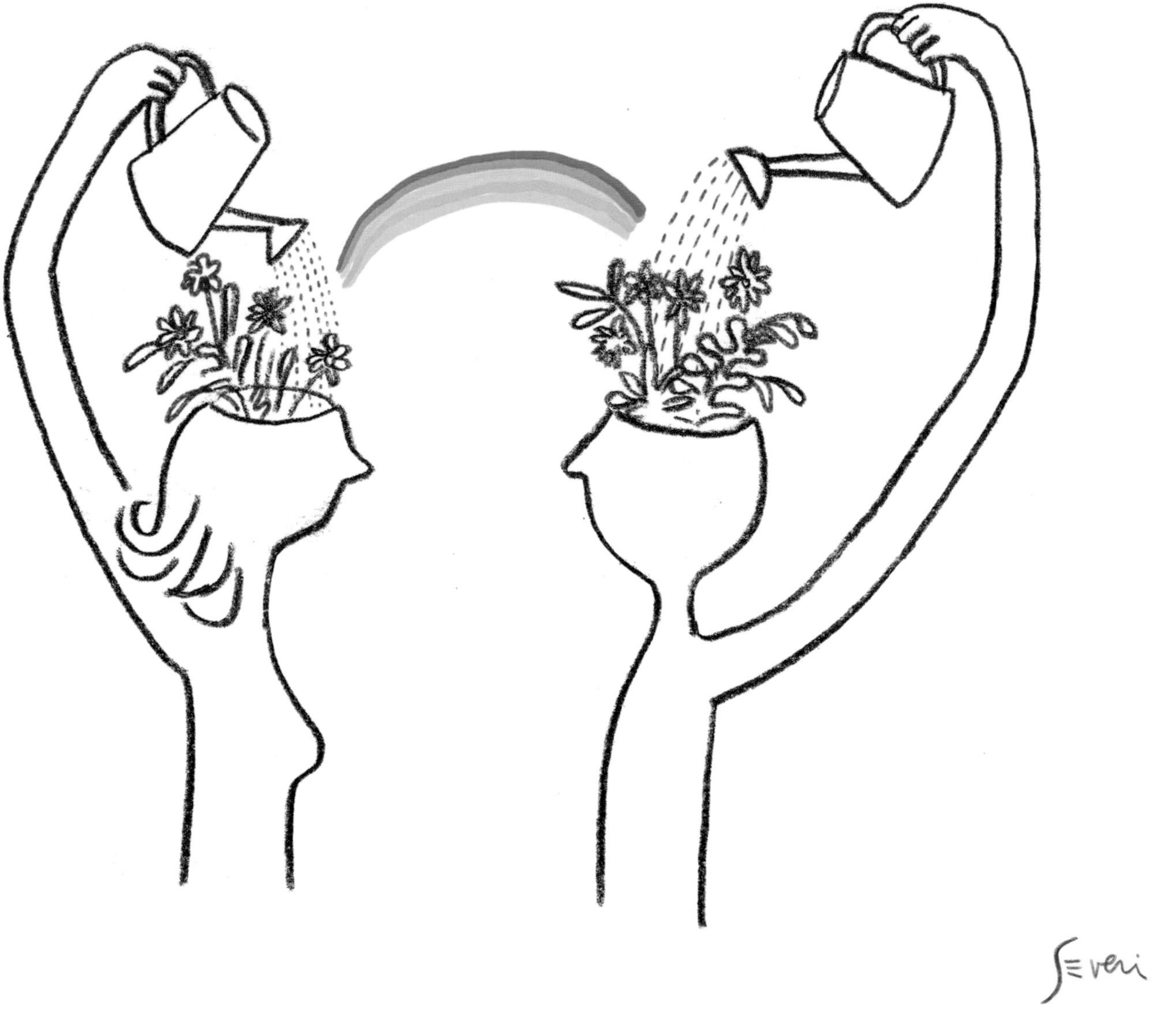
Severi

Severi

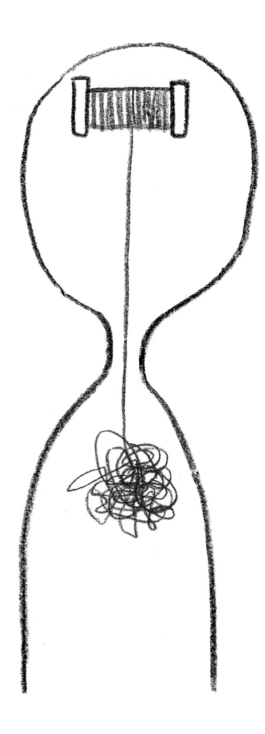

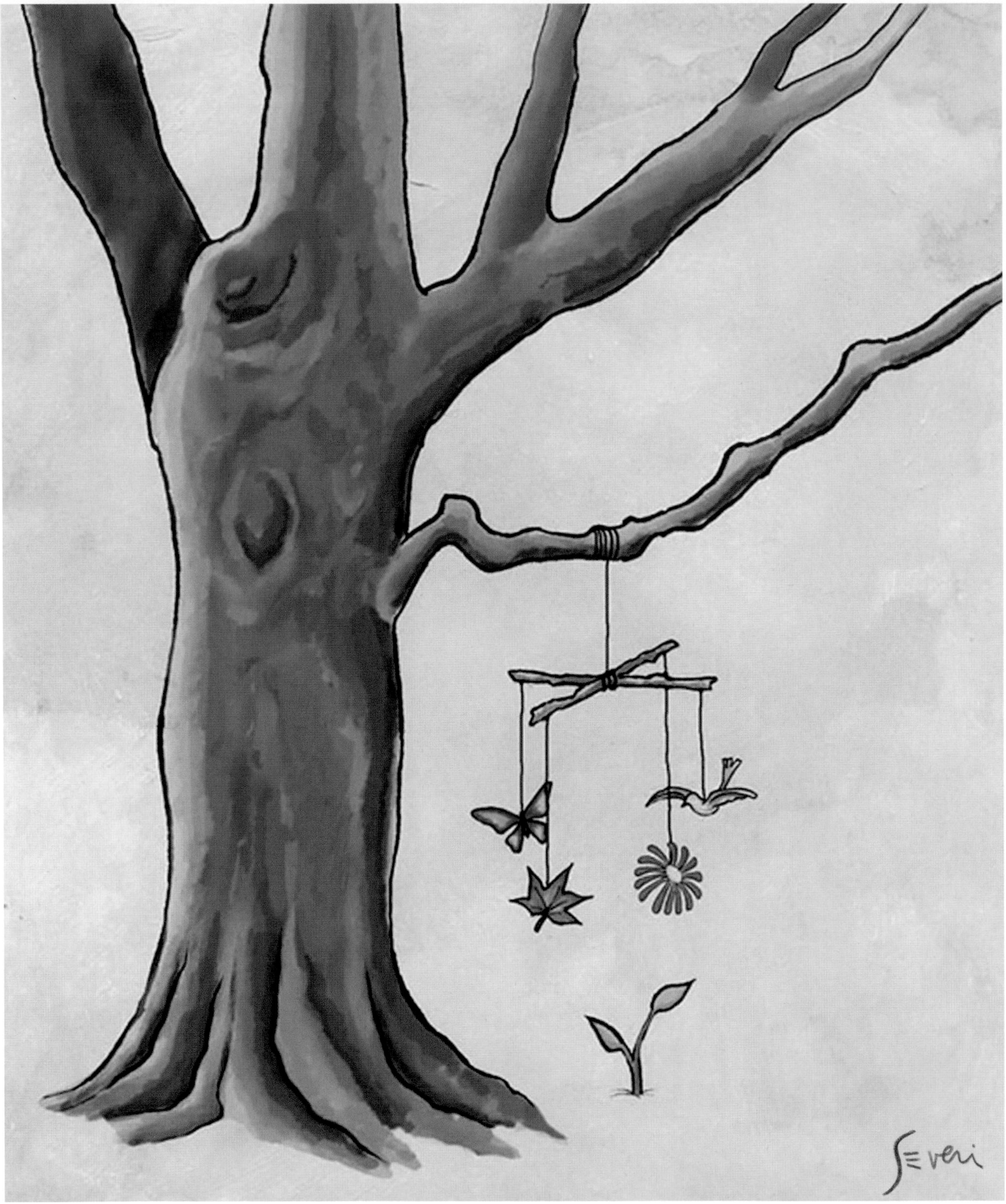
Severi

PAIN BRINGS US TOGETHER

Severi

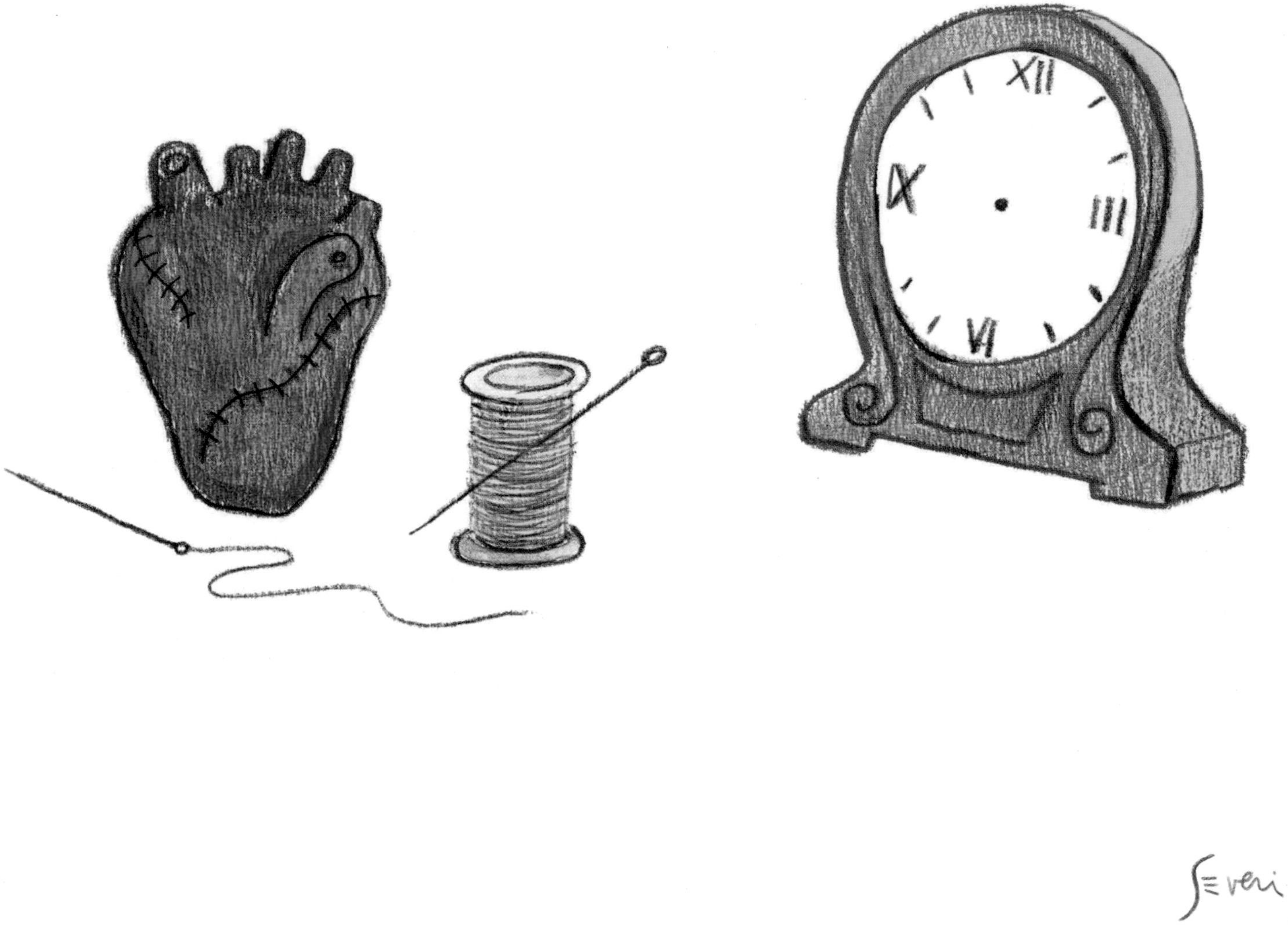
Severi

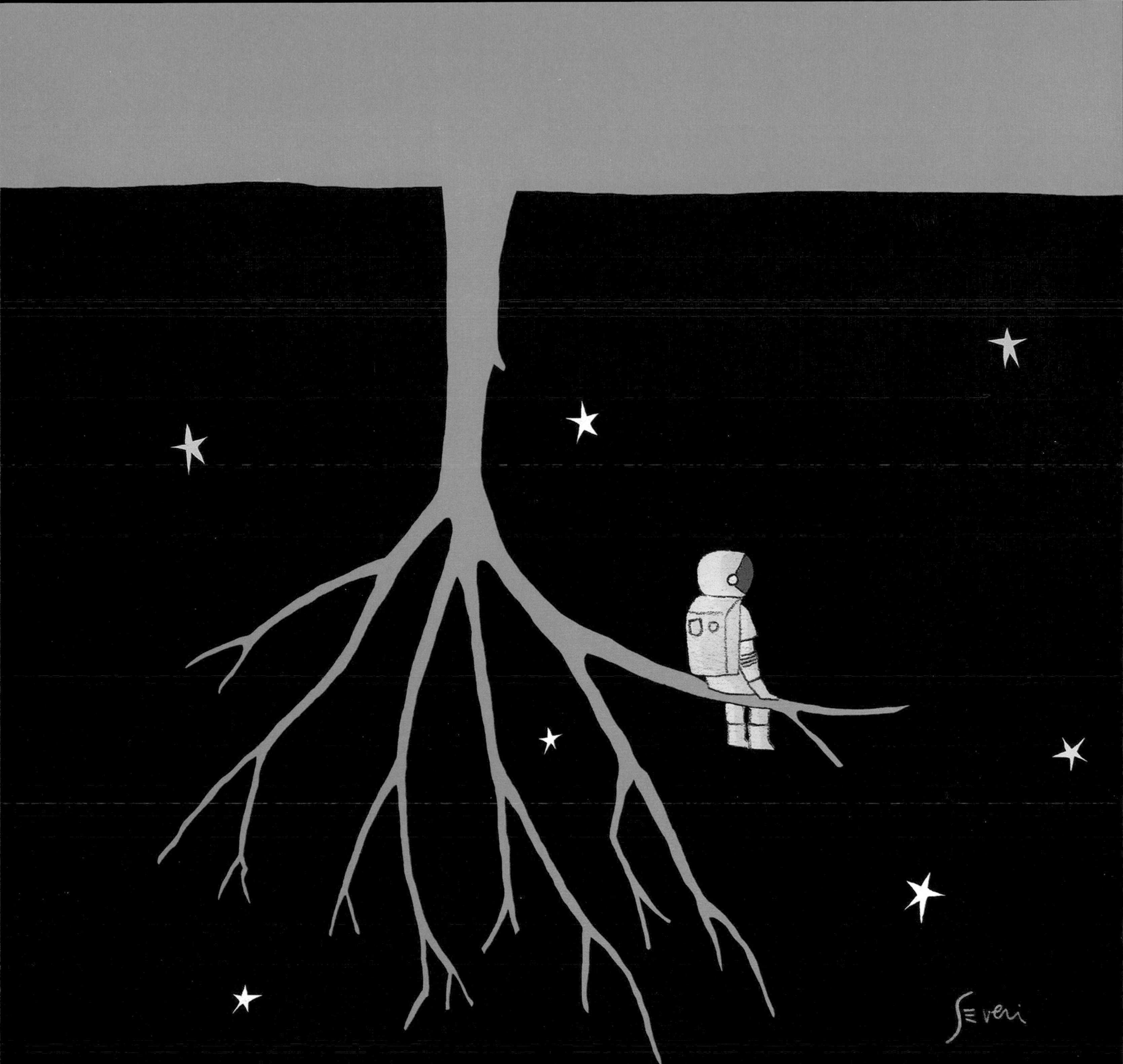

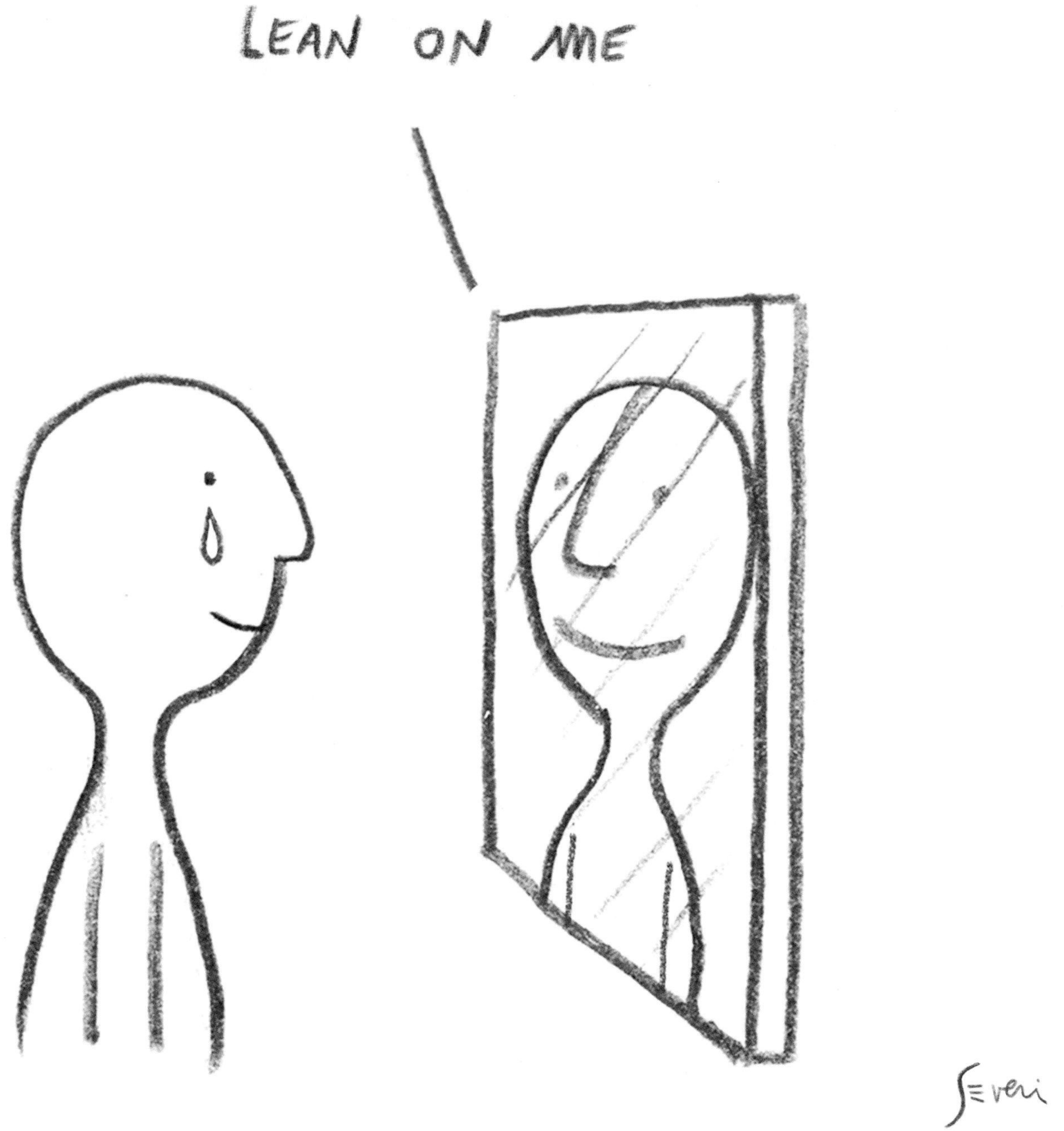
LEAN ON ME
Severi

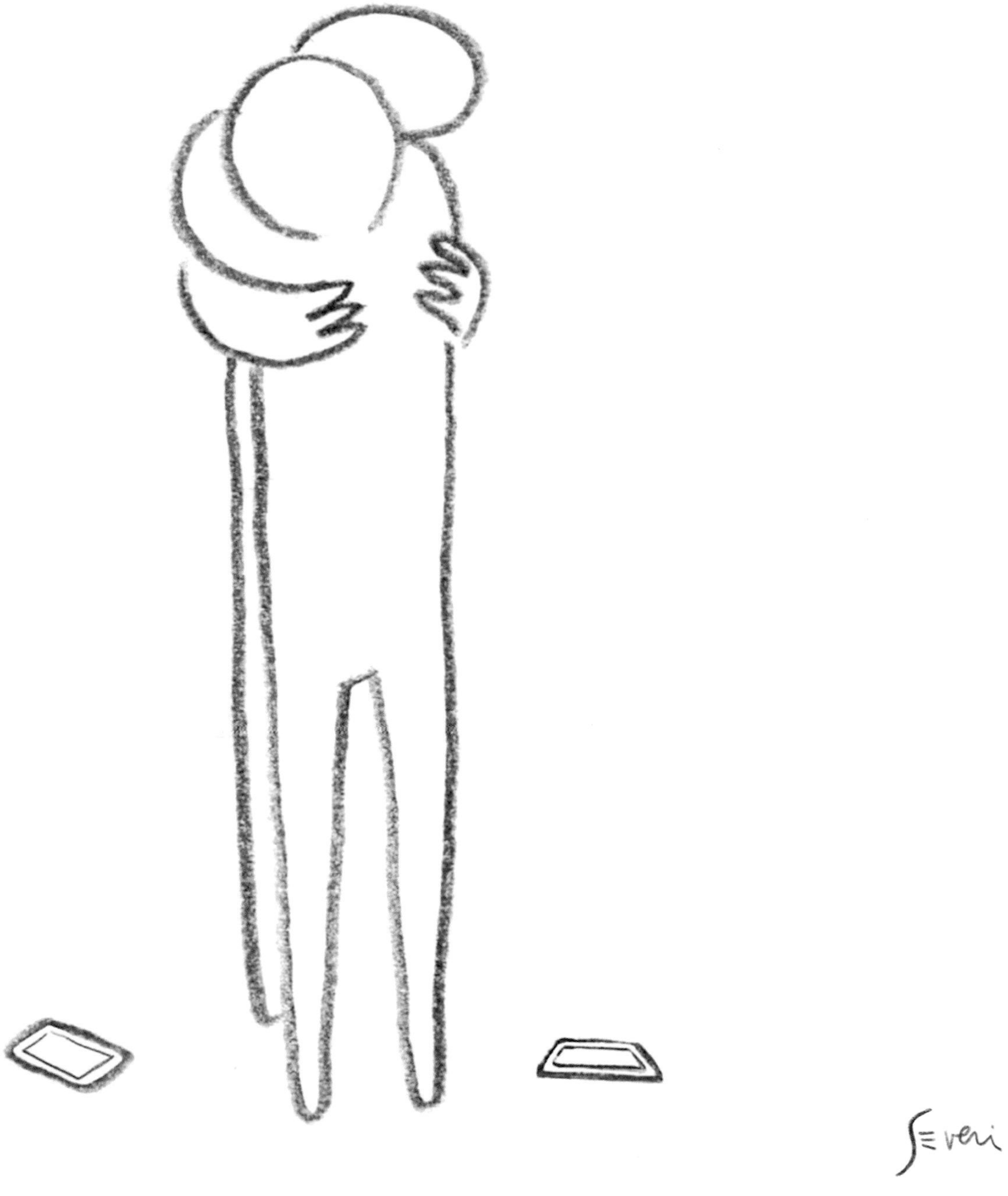
Severi

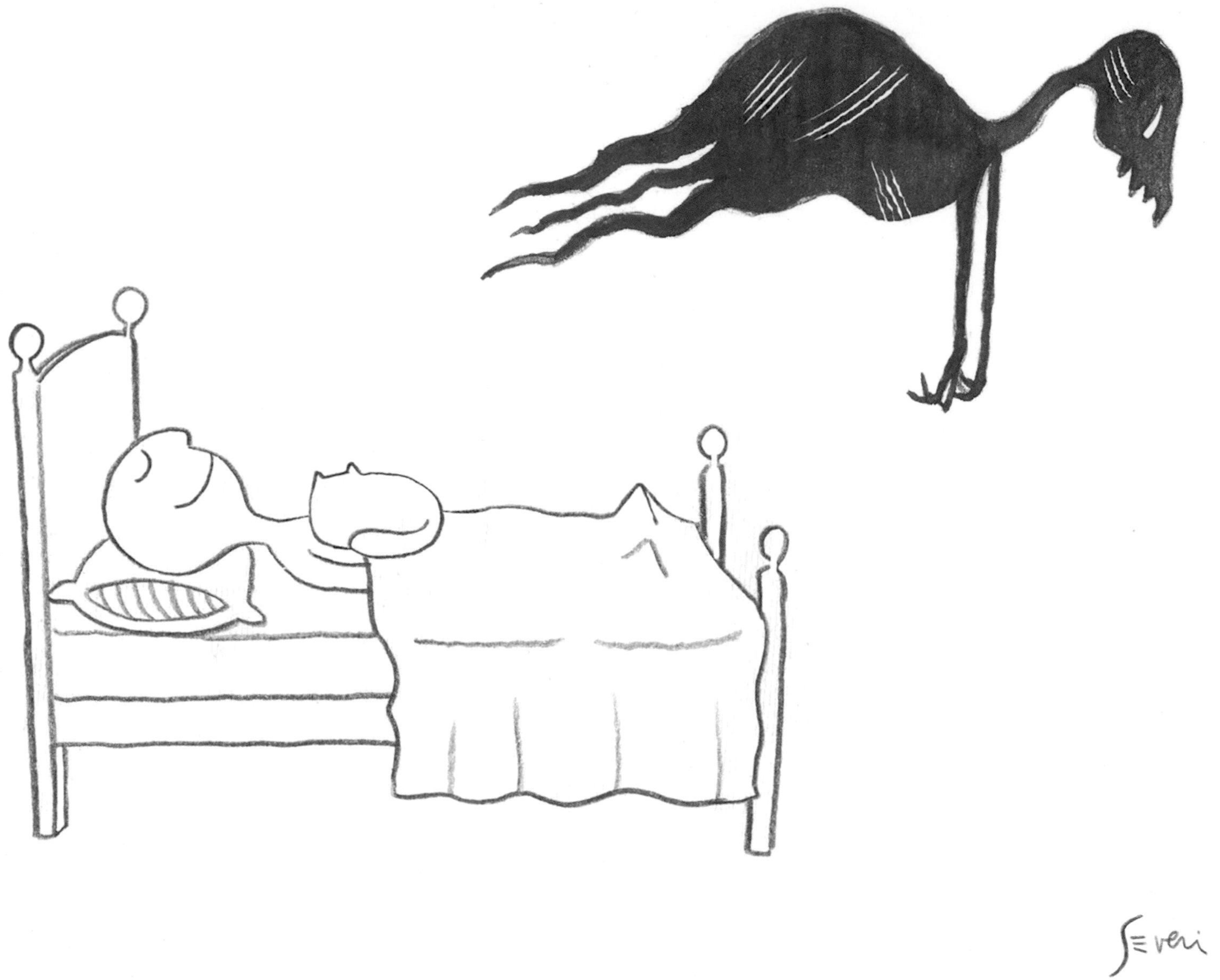

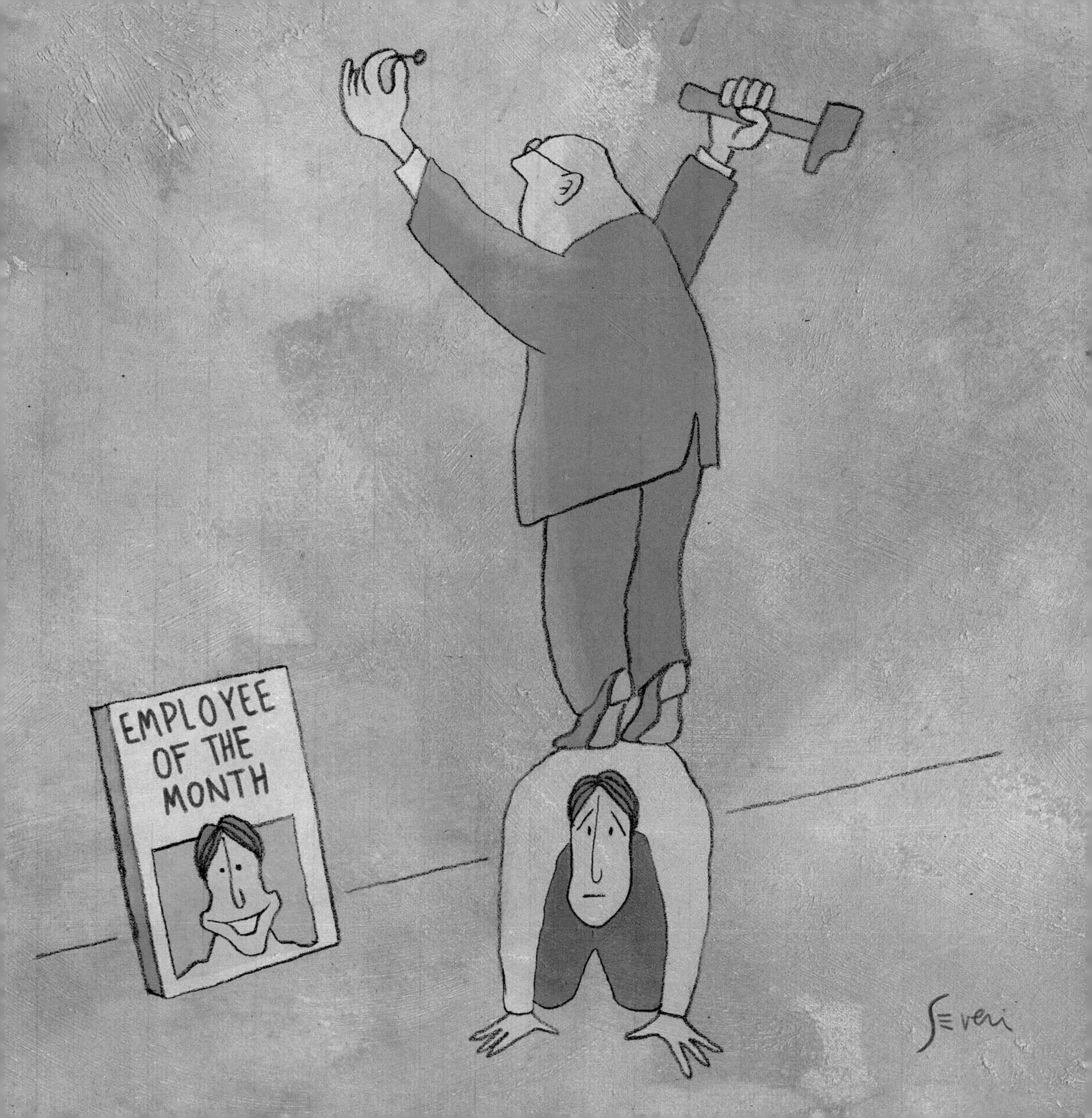
EMPLOYEE
OF THE
MONTH
Severi

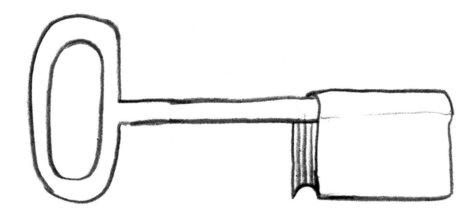

Severi

I DON'T SEE THINGS
THE WAY THEY ARE.
I SEE THEM
THE WAY I AM.

CAN I SHARE YOUR SOLITUDE?

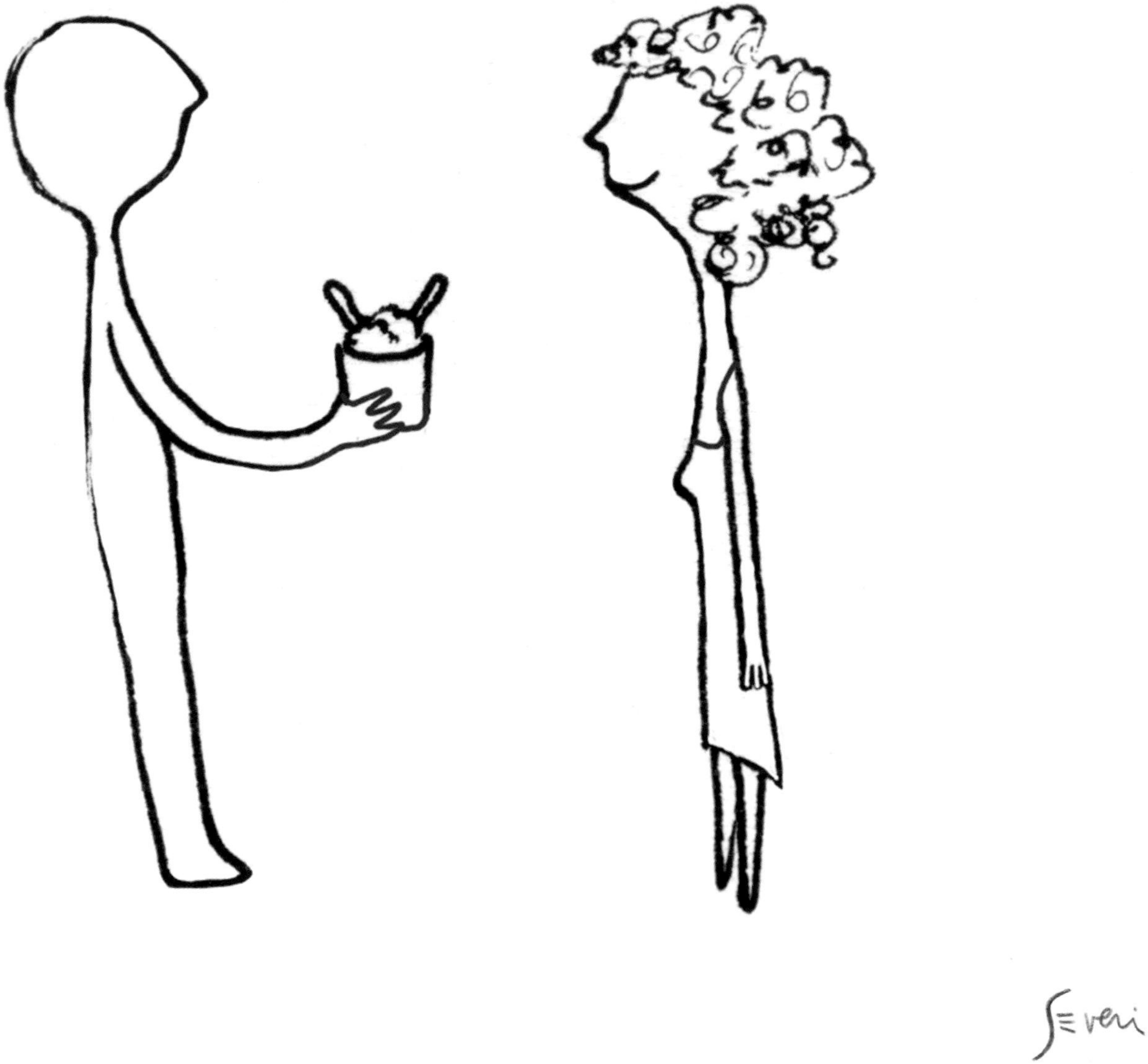
Severi

WHEN YOU ARE ON FIRE
NOTHING BURNS YOU.

Severi

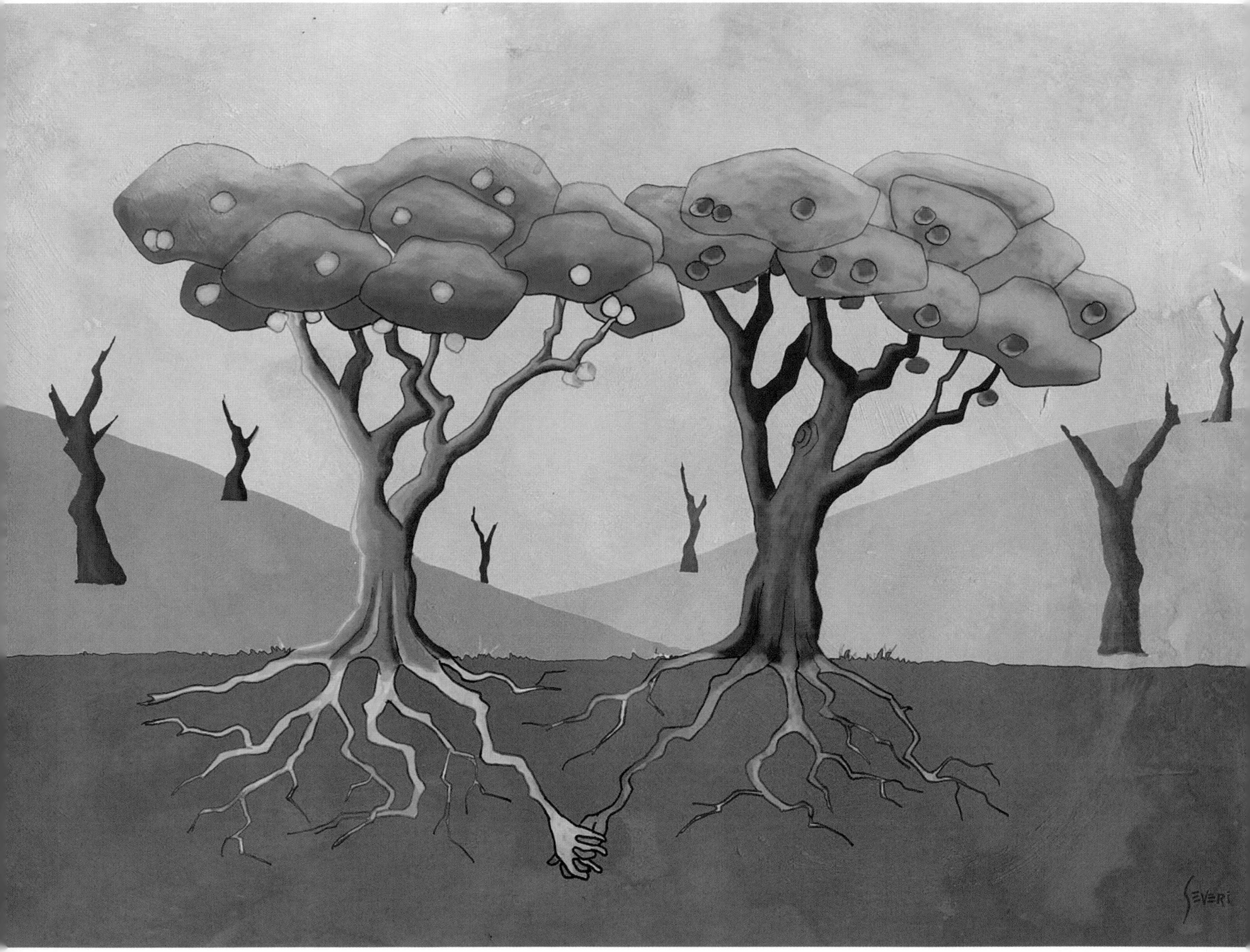
SEVERI

Severi

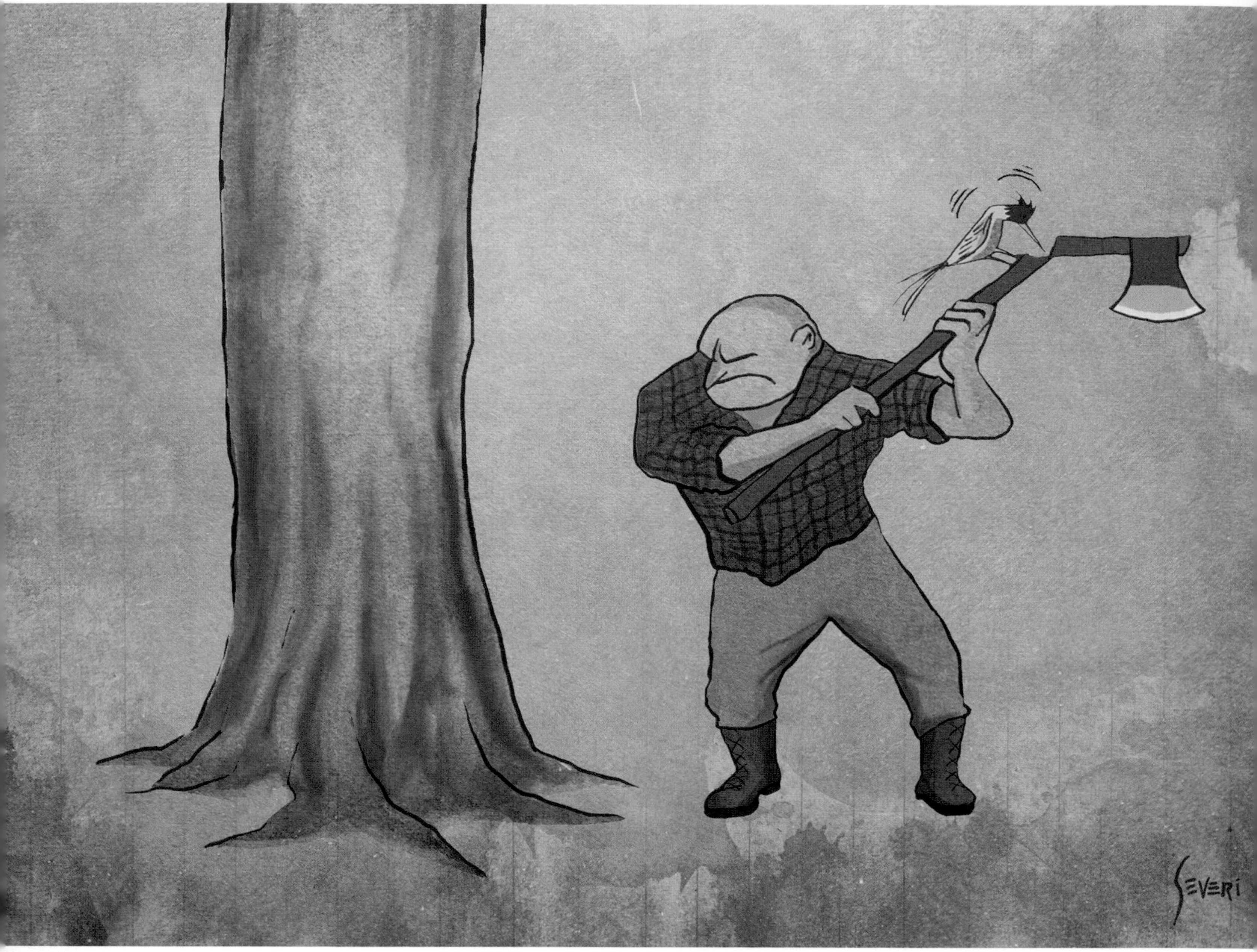
SEVERI

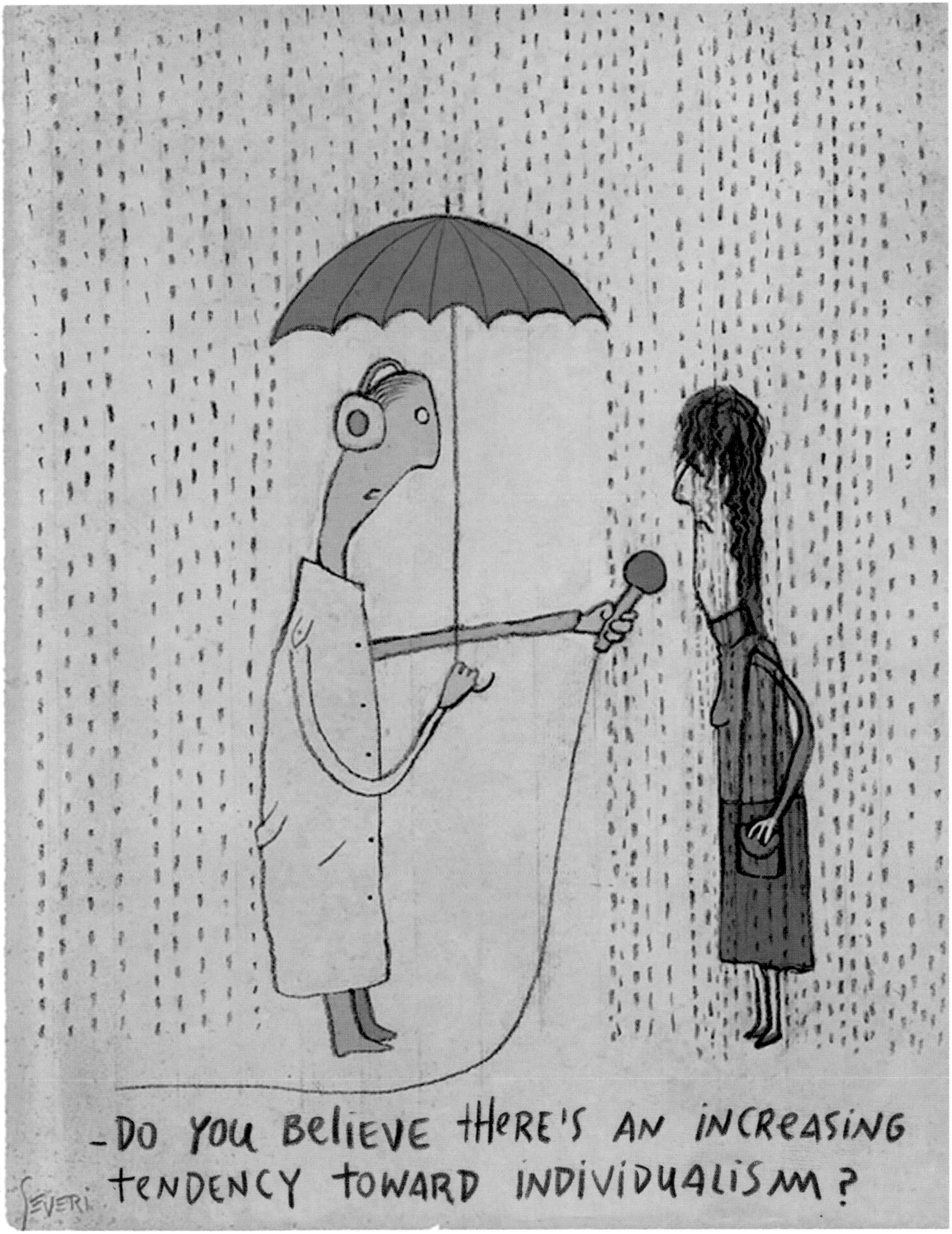

-DO YOU BELIEVE THERE'S AN INCREASING TENDENCY TOWARD INDIVIDUALISM?
SEVERI

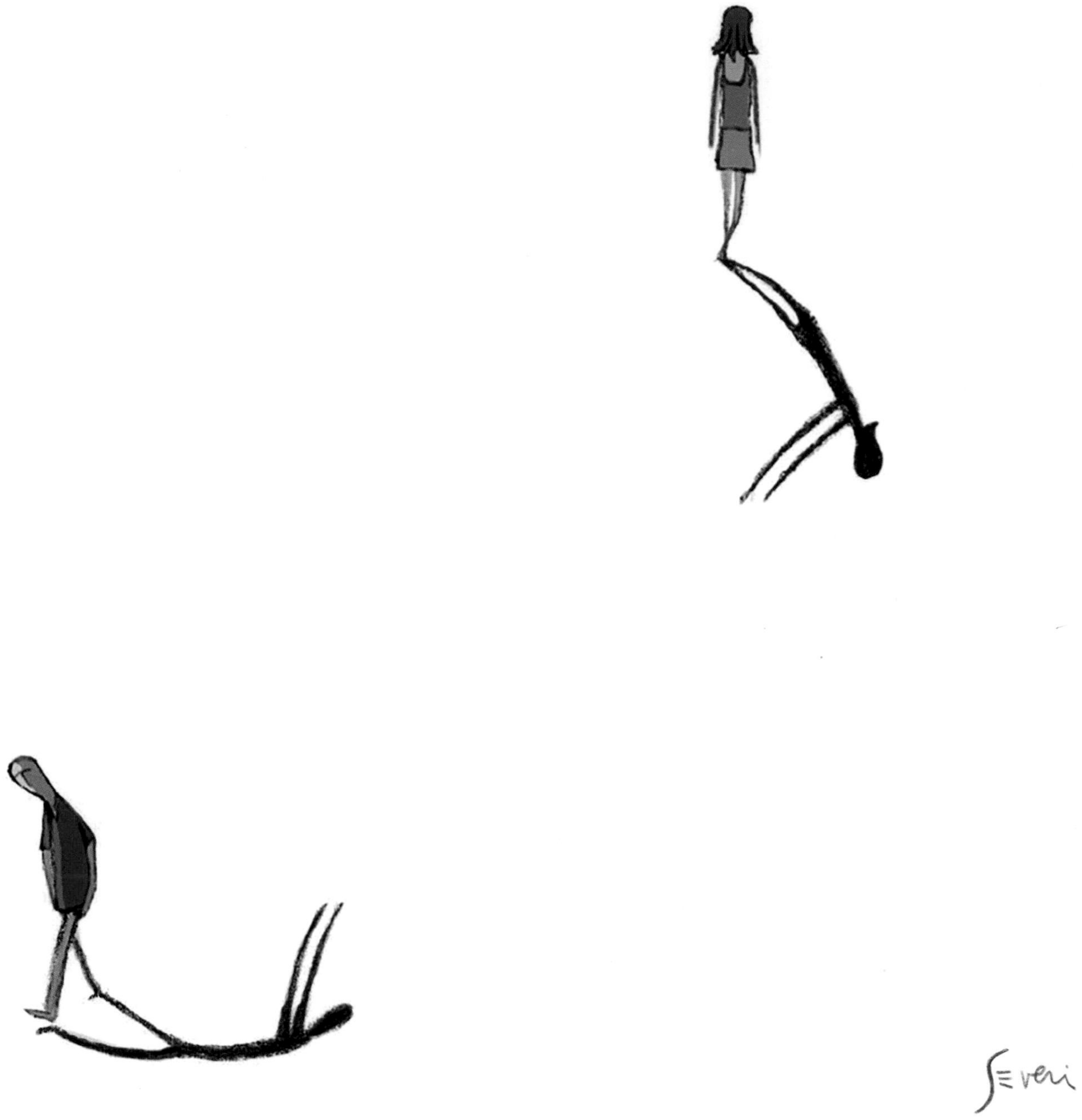
Severi

EXPOSER OF TRUTH

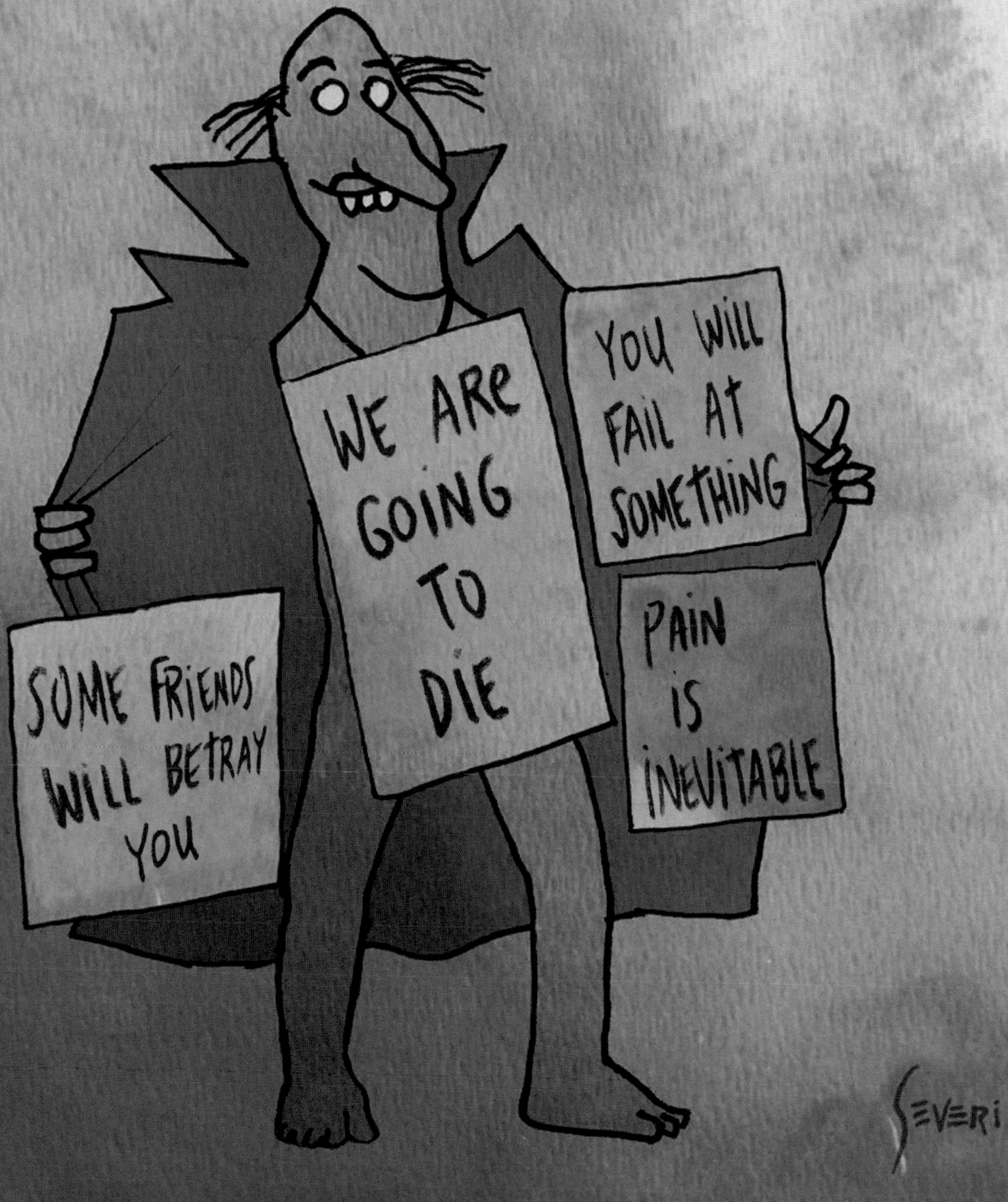

WE ARE GOING TO DIE
YOU WILL FAIL AT SOMETHING
PAIN IS INEVITABLE
SOME FRIENDS WILL BETRAY YOU
SEVERI

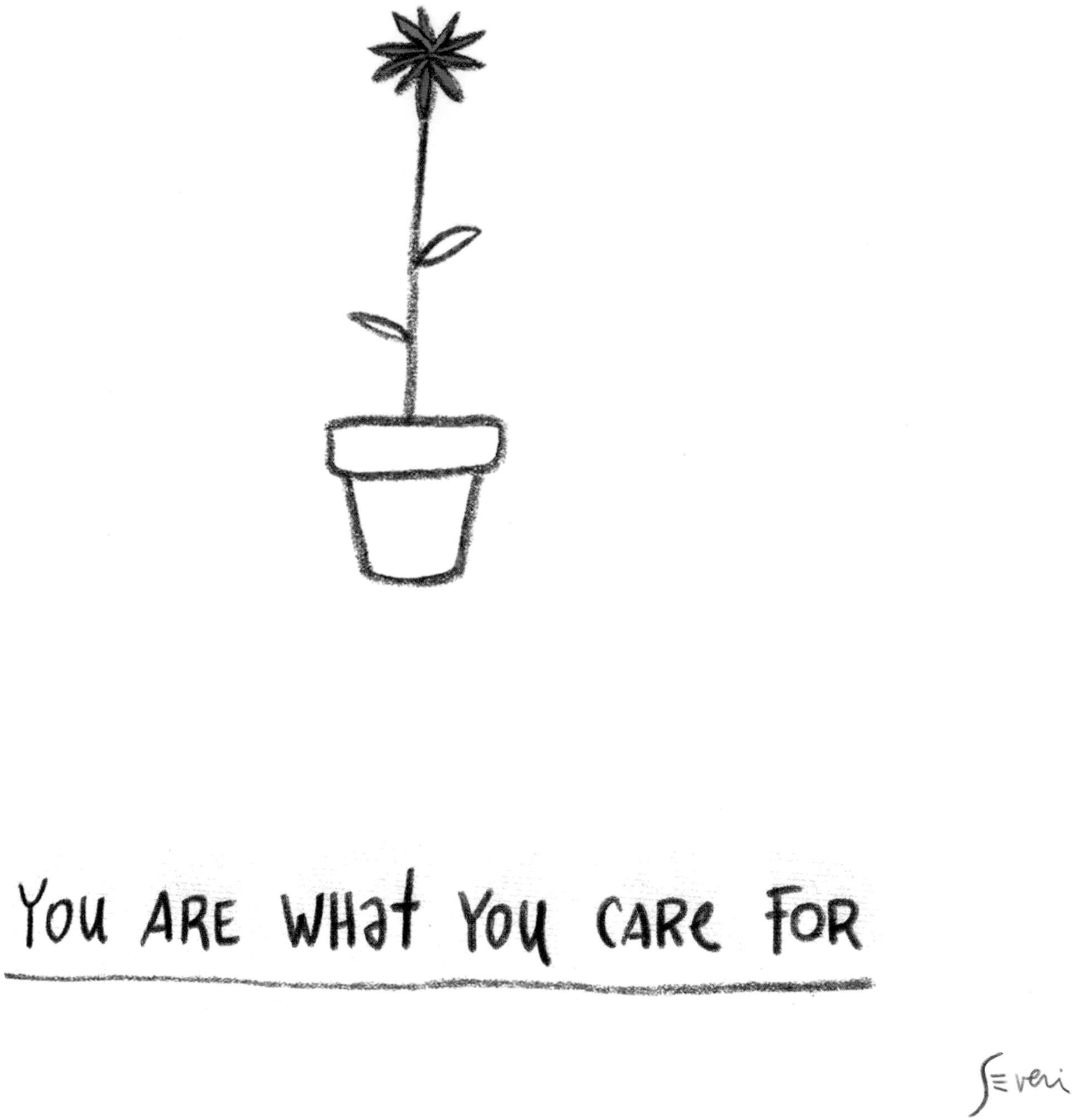
YOU ARE WHAT YOU CARE FOR
Severi

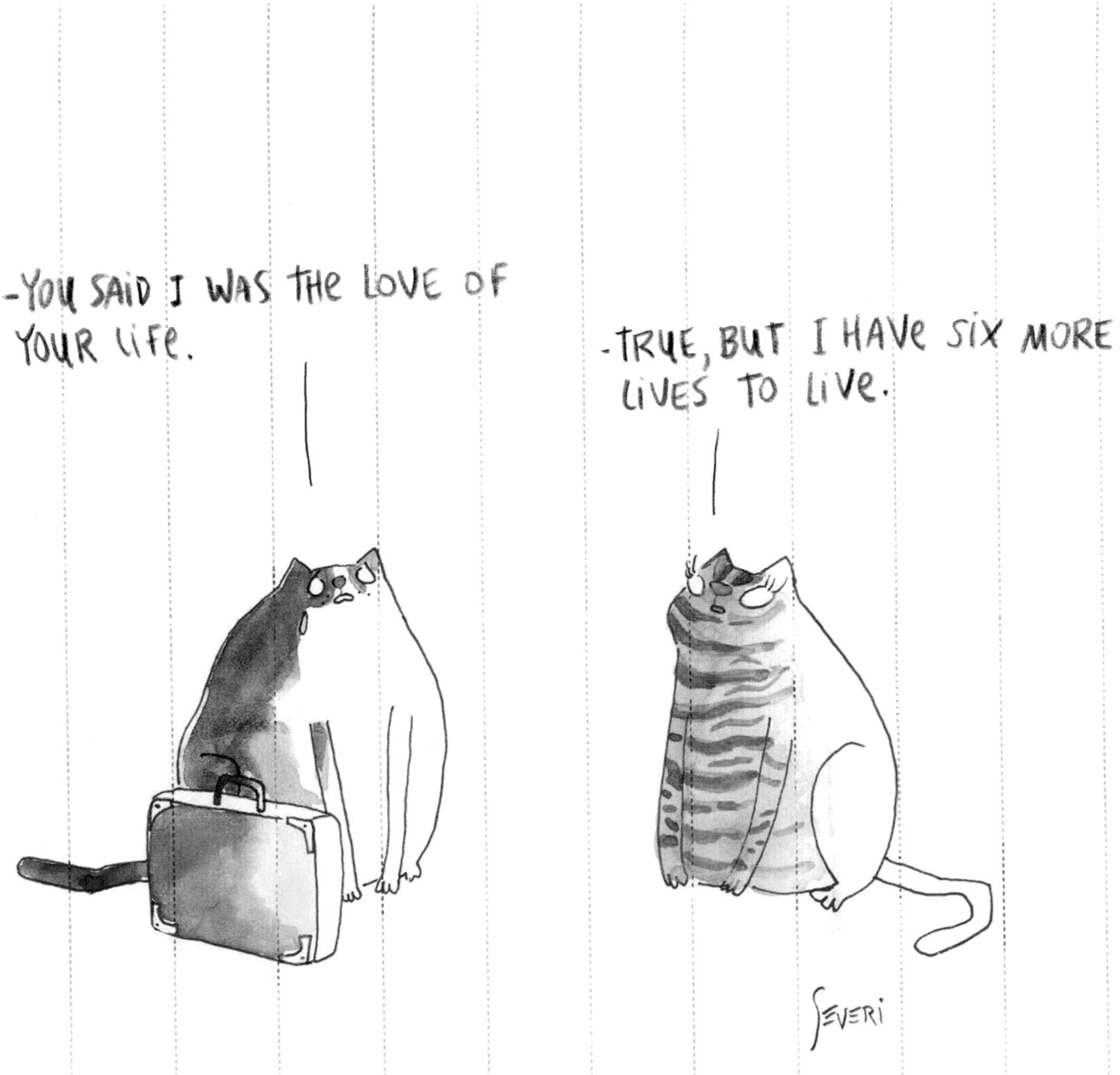
-YOU SAID I WAS THE LOVE OF YOUR LIFE.
-TRUE, BUT I HAVE SIX MORE LIVES TO LIVE.
SEVERI

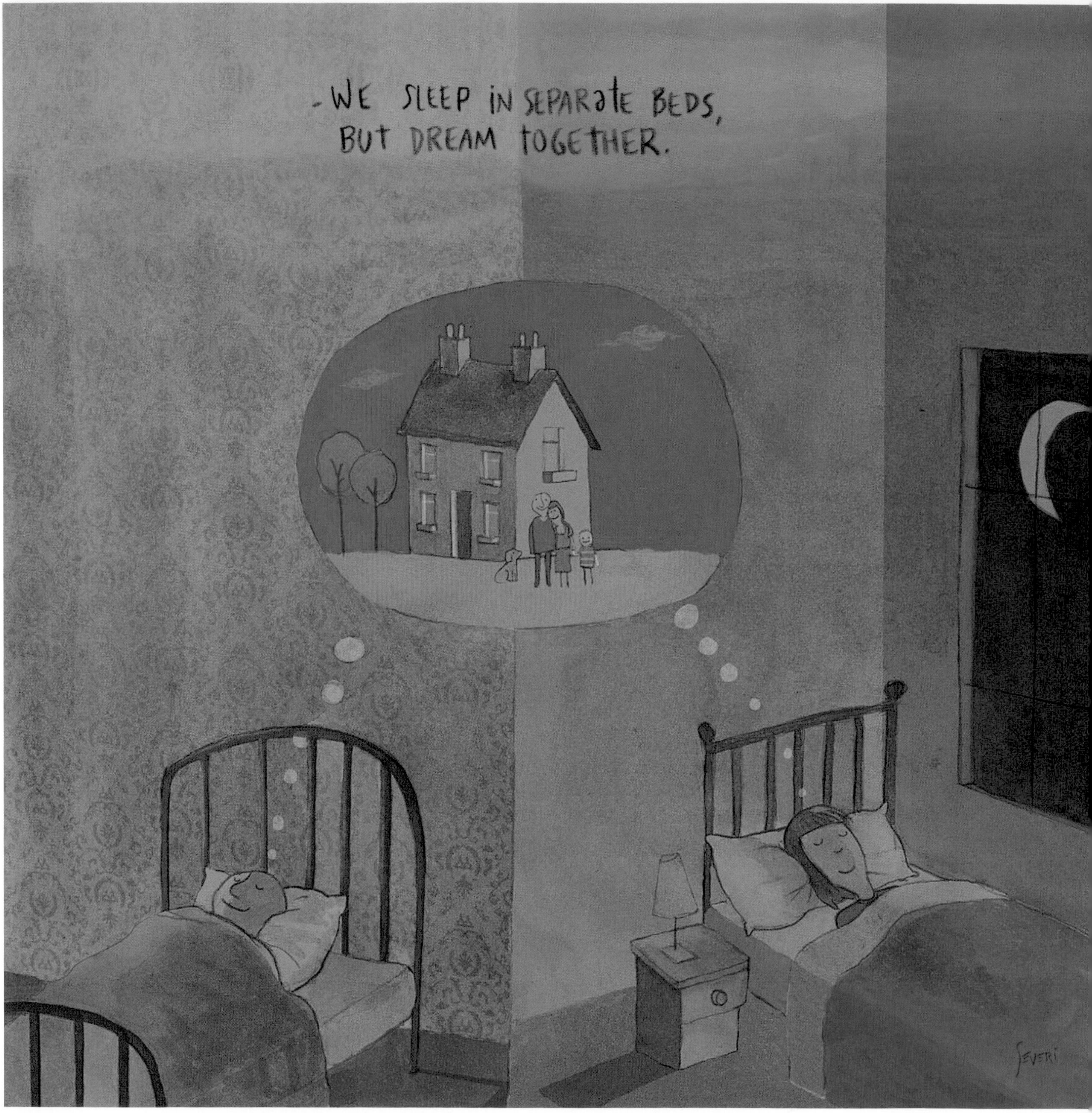
-WE SLEEP IN SEPARATE BEDS,
BUT DREAM TOGETHER.
SEVERI

Severi

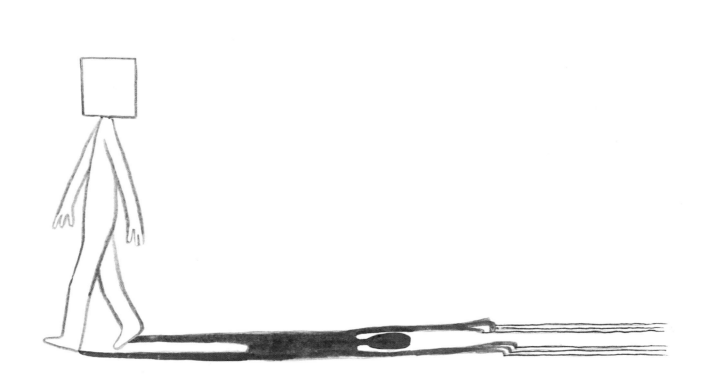

A HUG AND A DRAWING
HAVE SOMETHING IN
COMMON:

THEY REACH PLACES WORDS
CAN NOT.

Severi

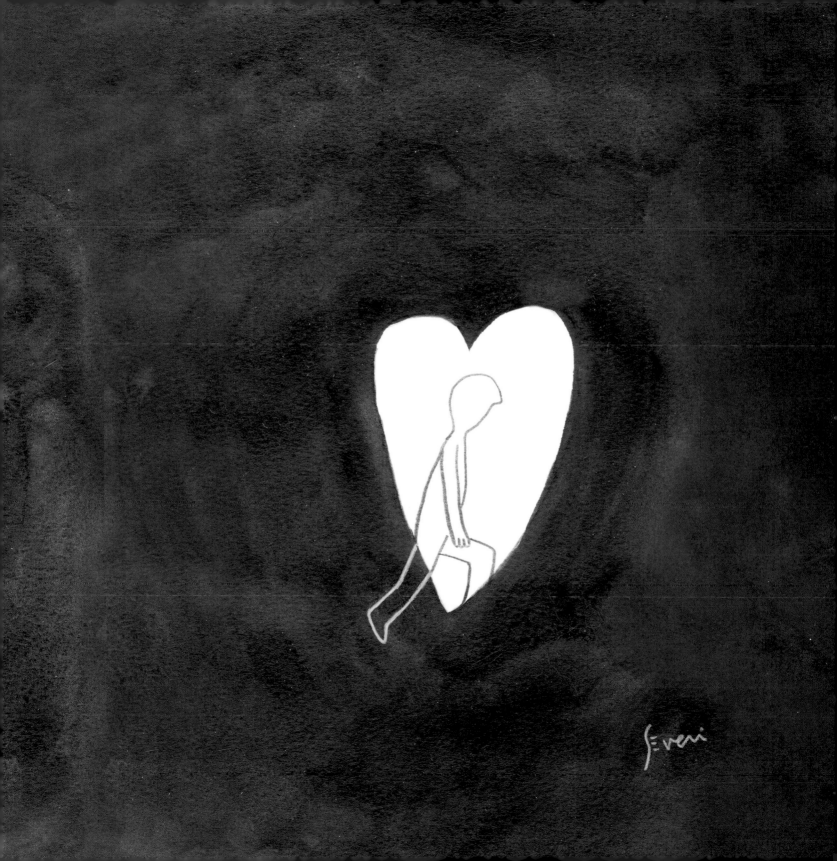

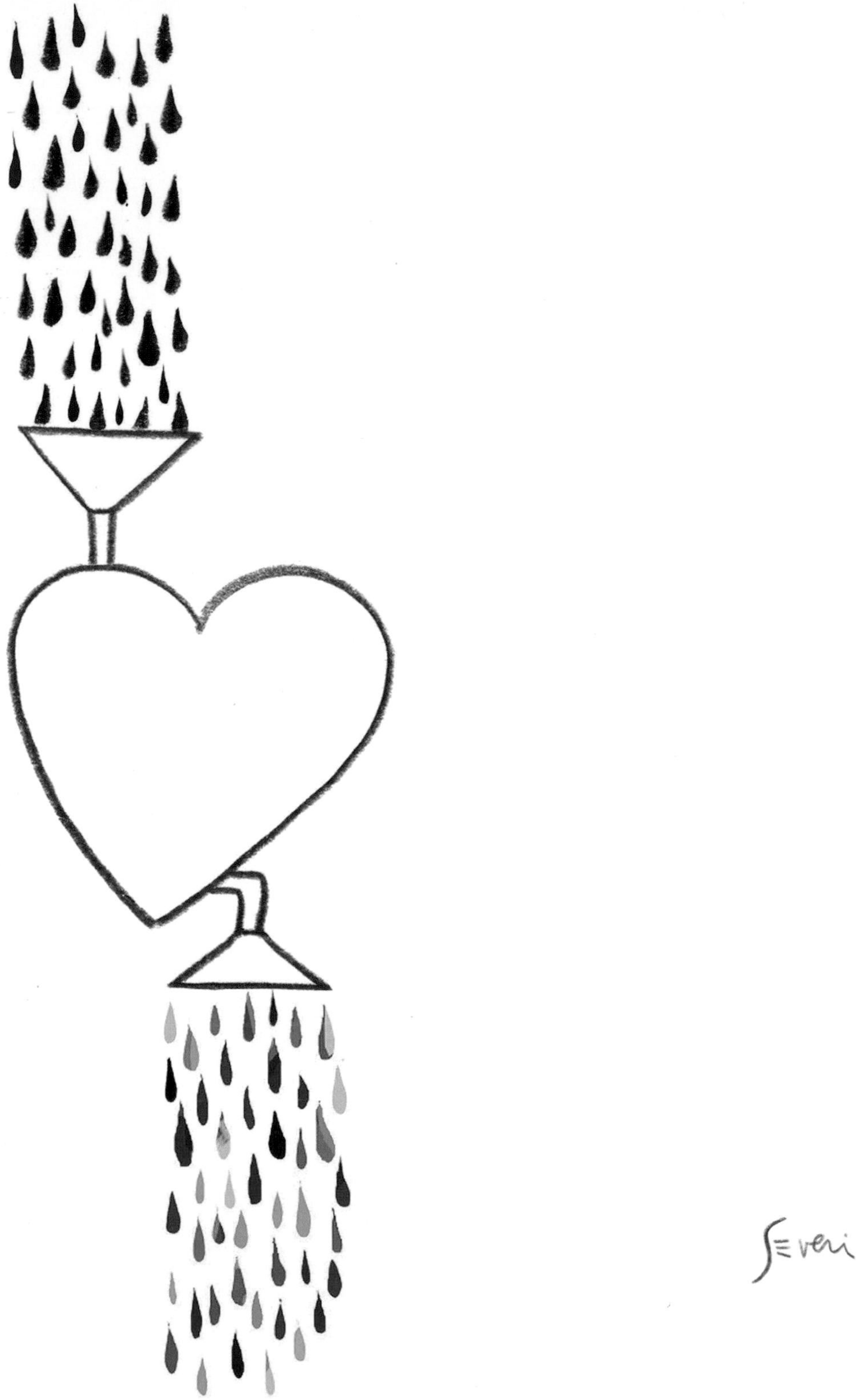
Severi

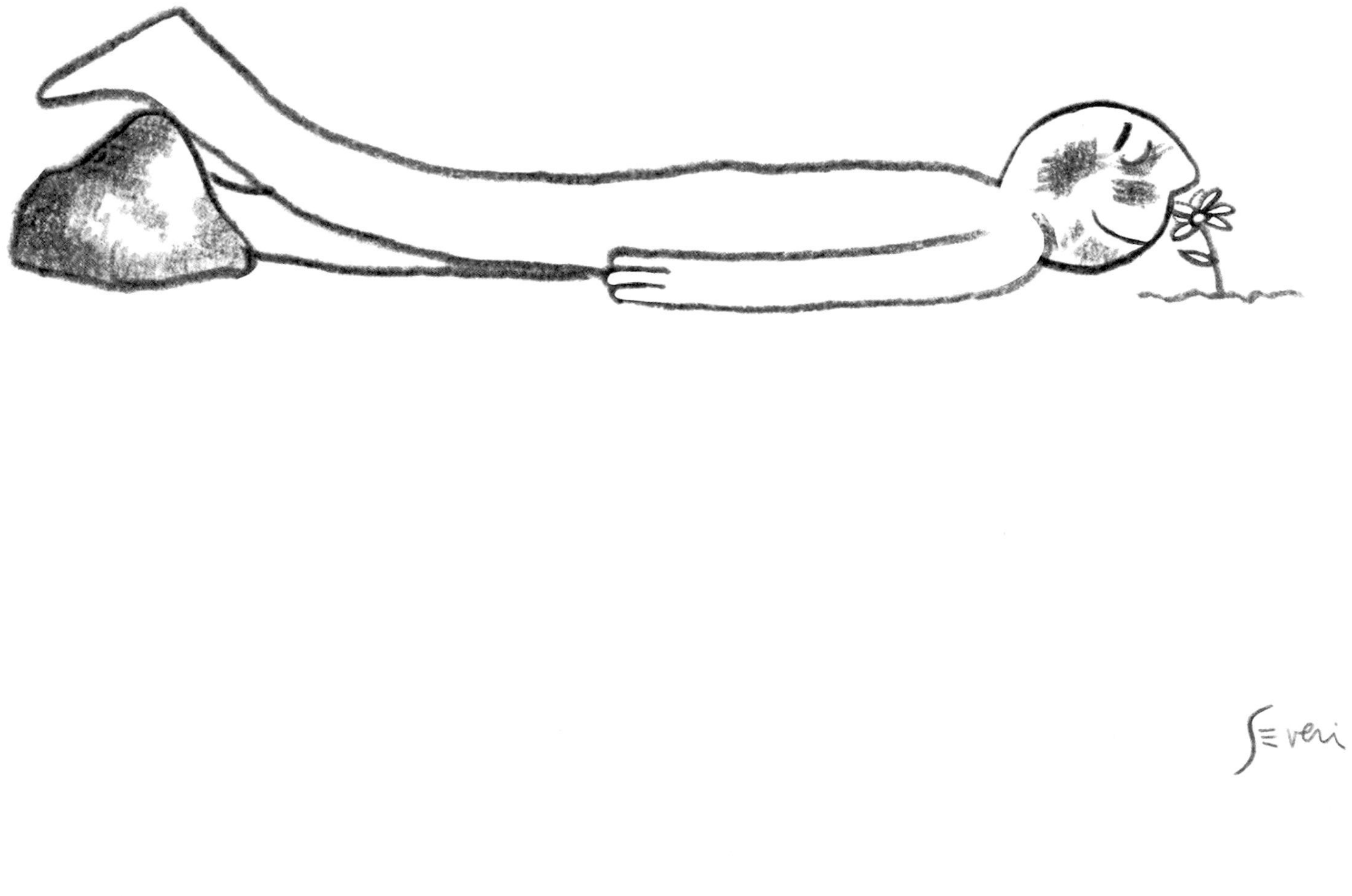
Severi

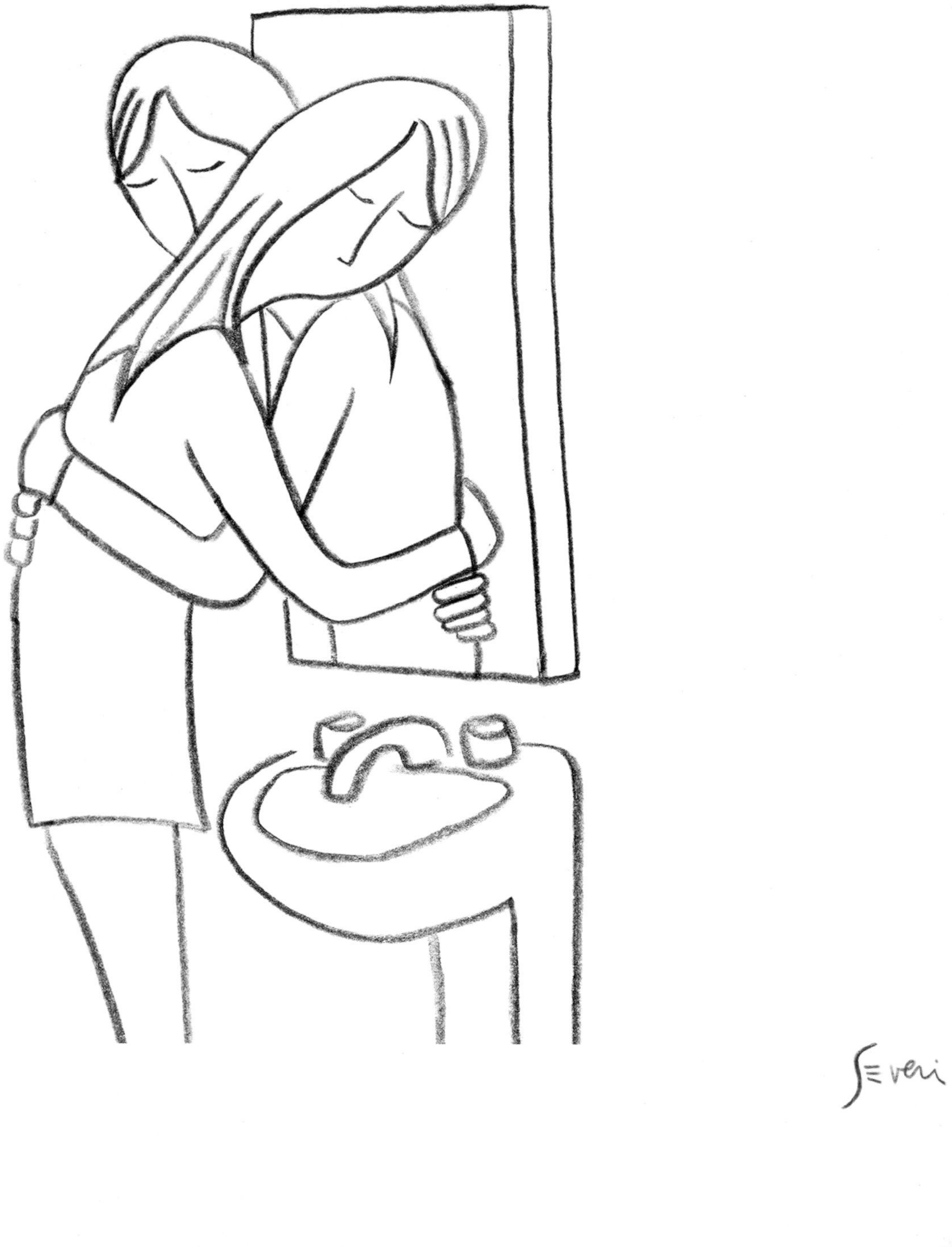
Severi

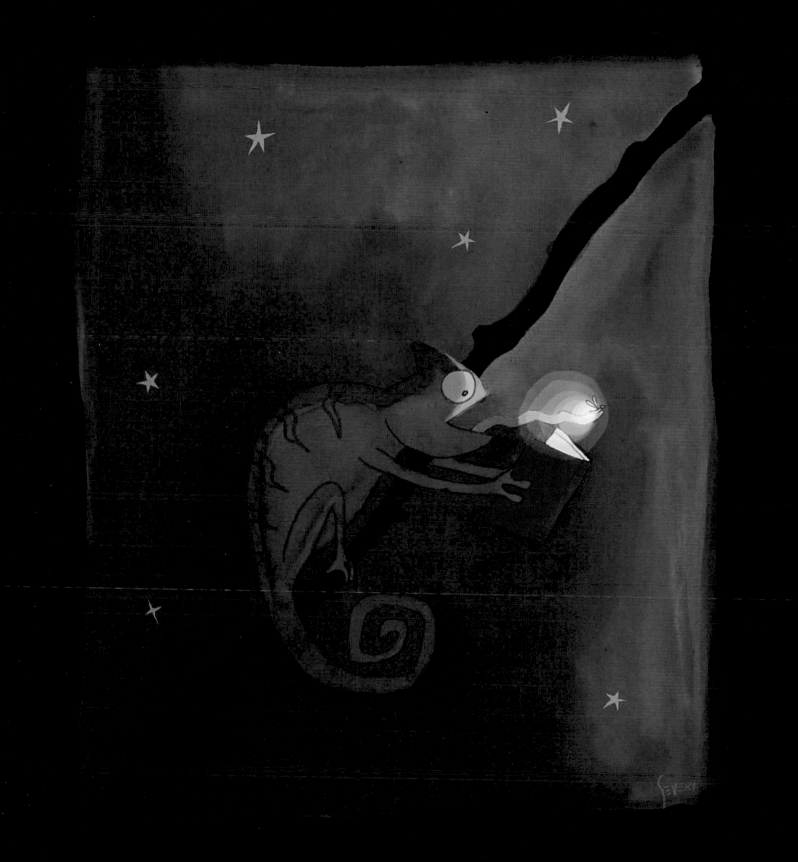

WITH POETRY EVERYTHING IS NOVEL

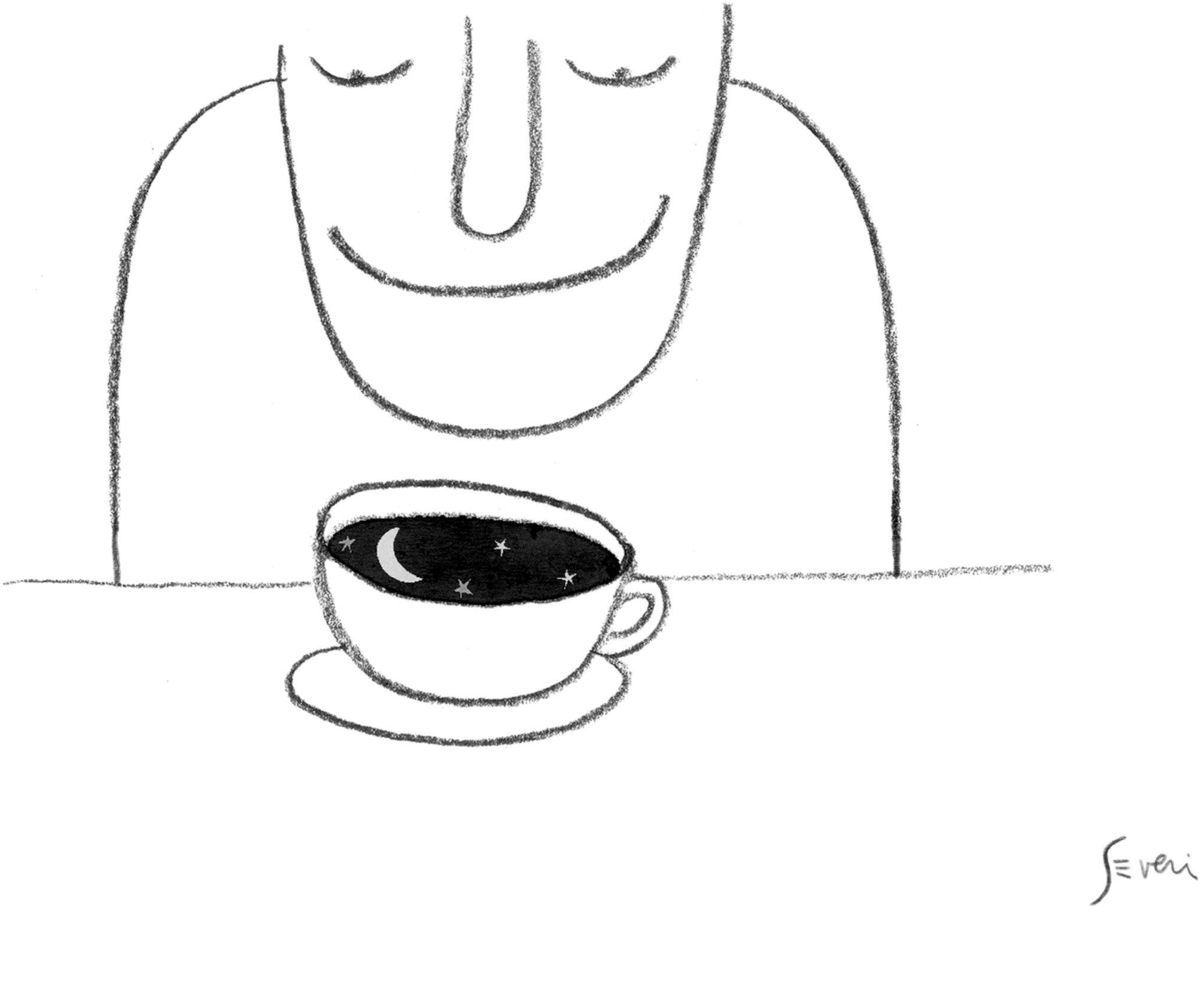
Severi

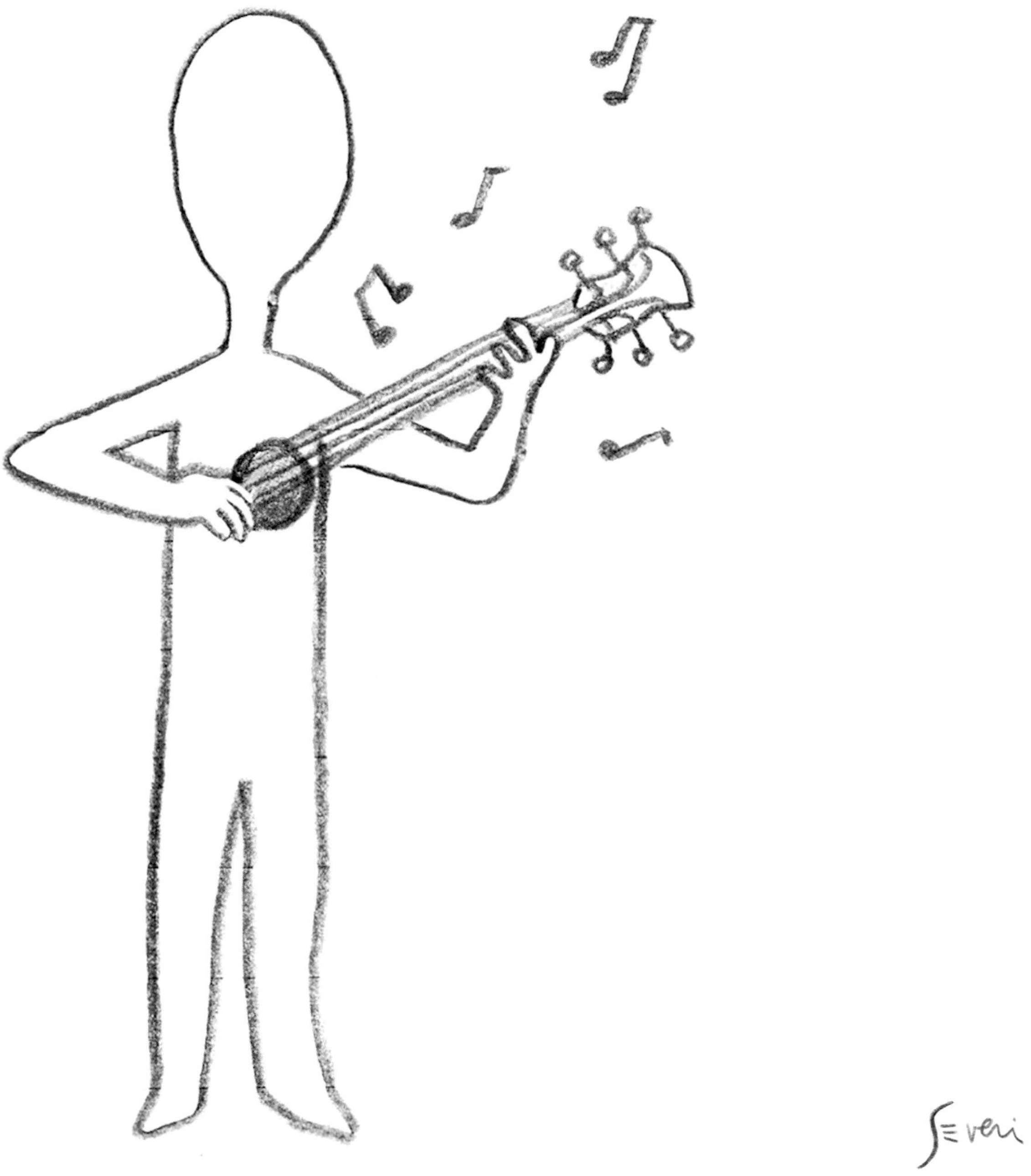
Severi

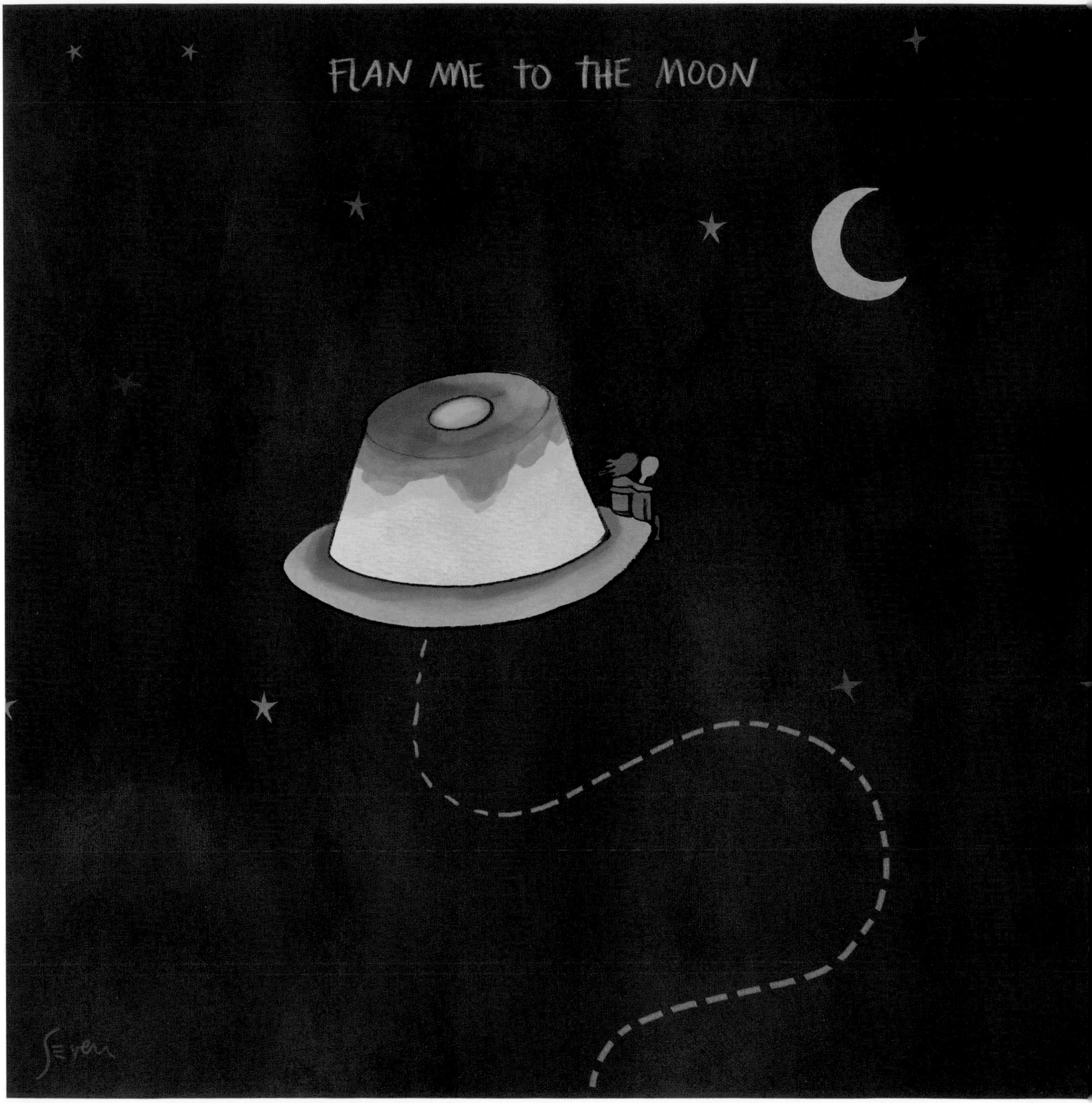
FLAN ME TO THE MOON
Severi

YOU MARVELED LIKE A KID...

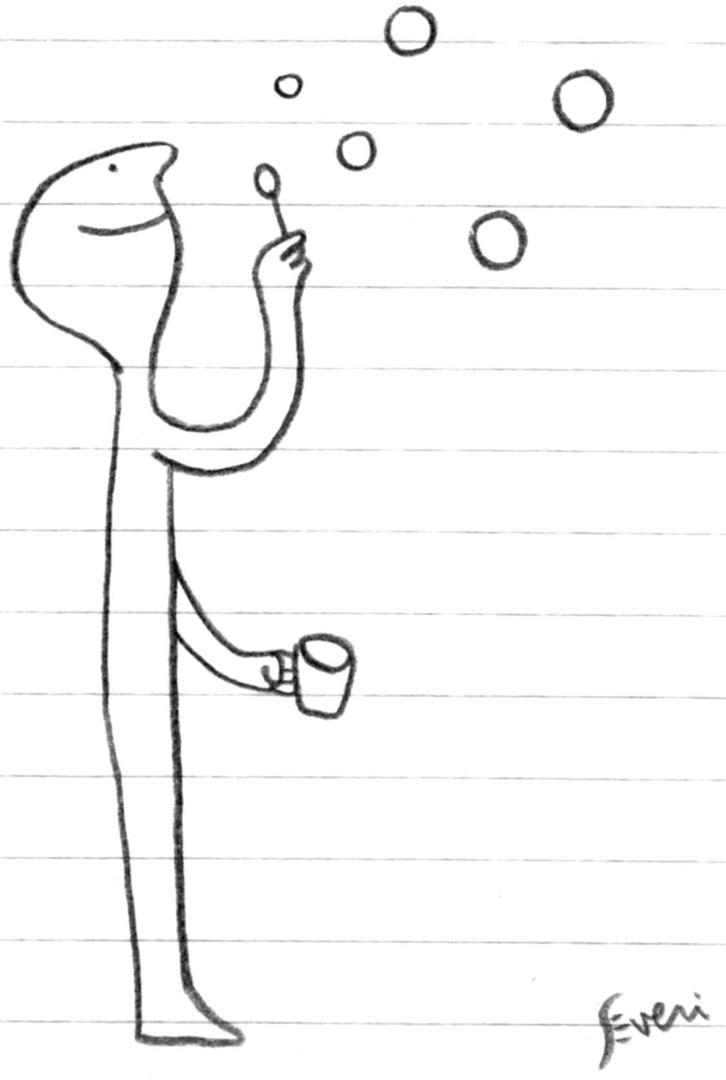

YOU'VE GROWN.

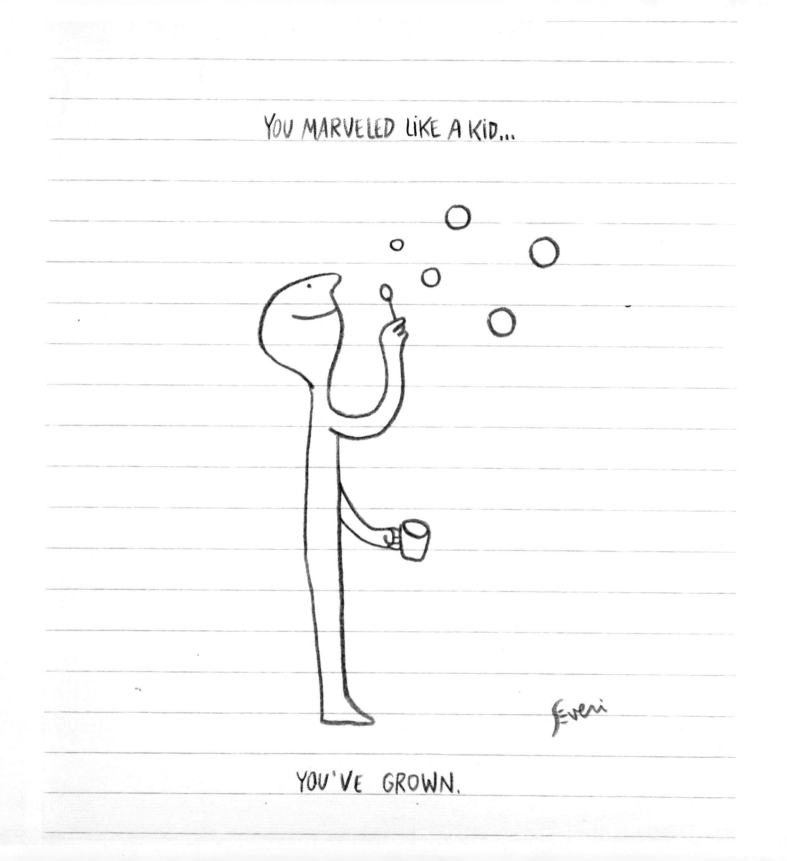

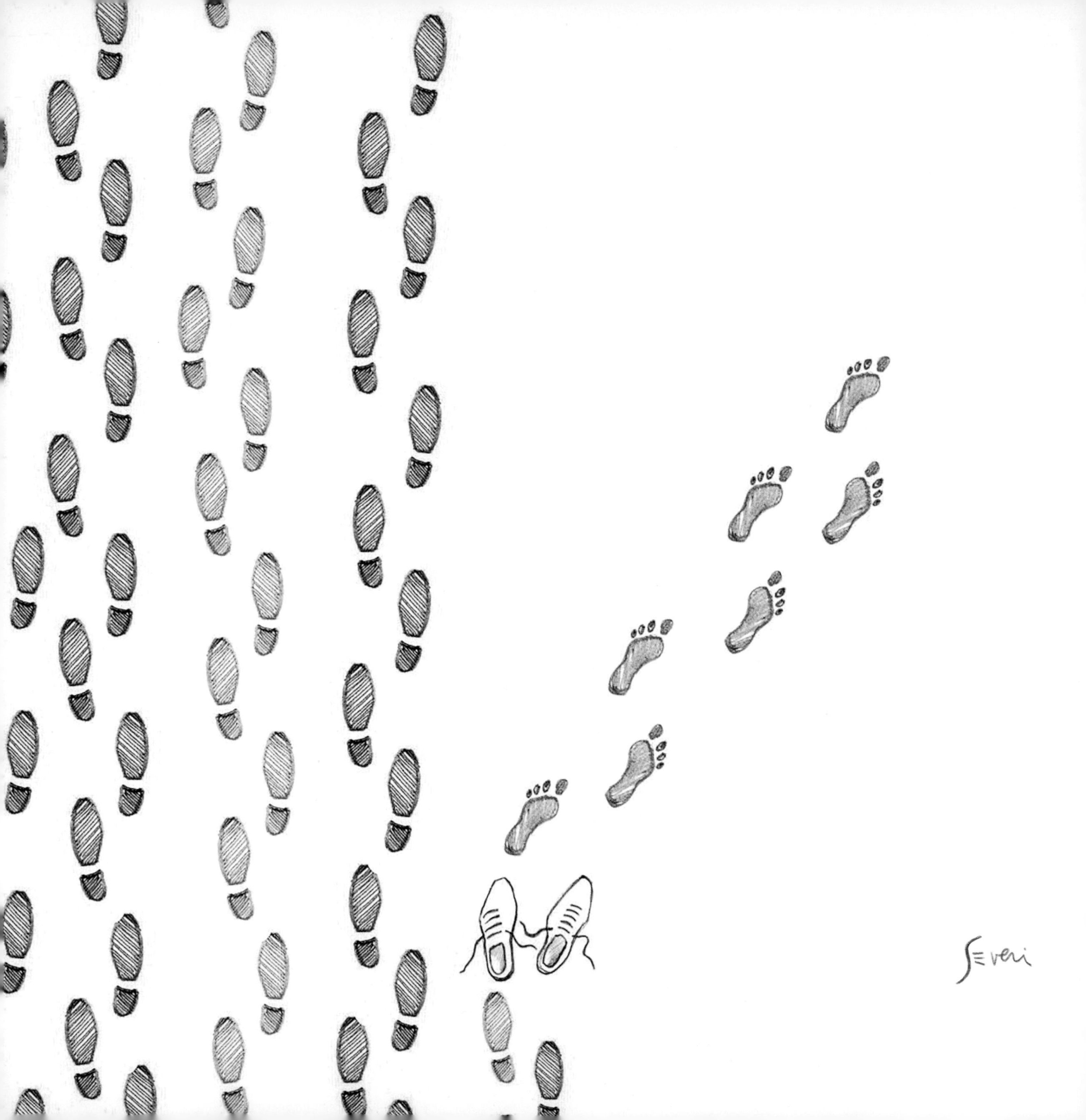
Severi

WE ARE FRESH OUT OF SWEET CHILDHOOD MEMORIES, BUT WE DO HAVE BLAND AUTOPILOT OR BITTER EXISTENCIAL CRISIS

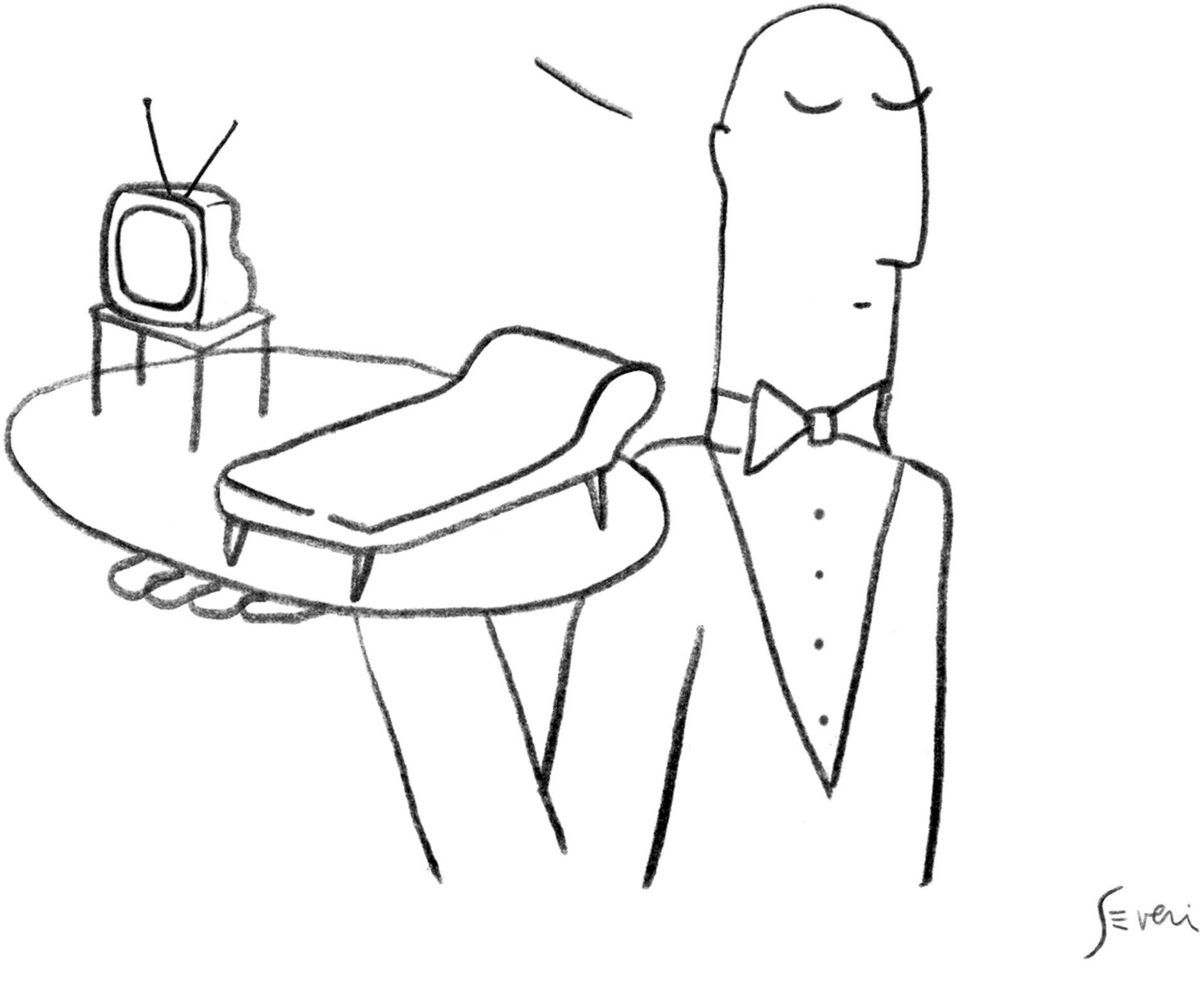
Severi

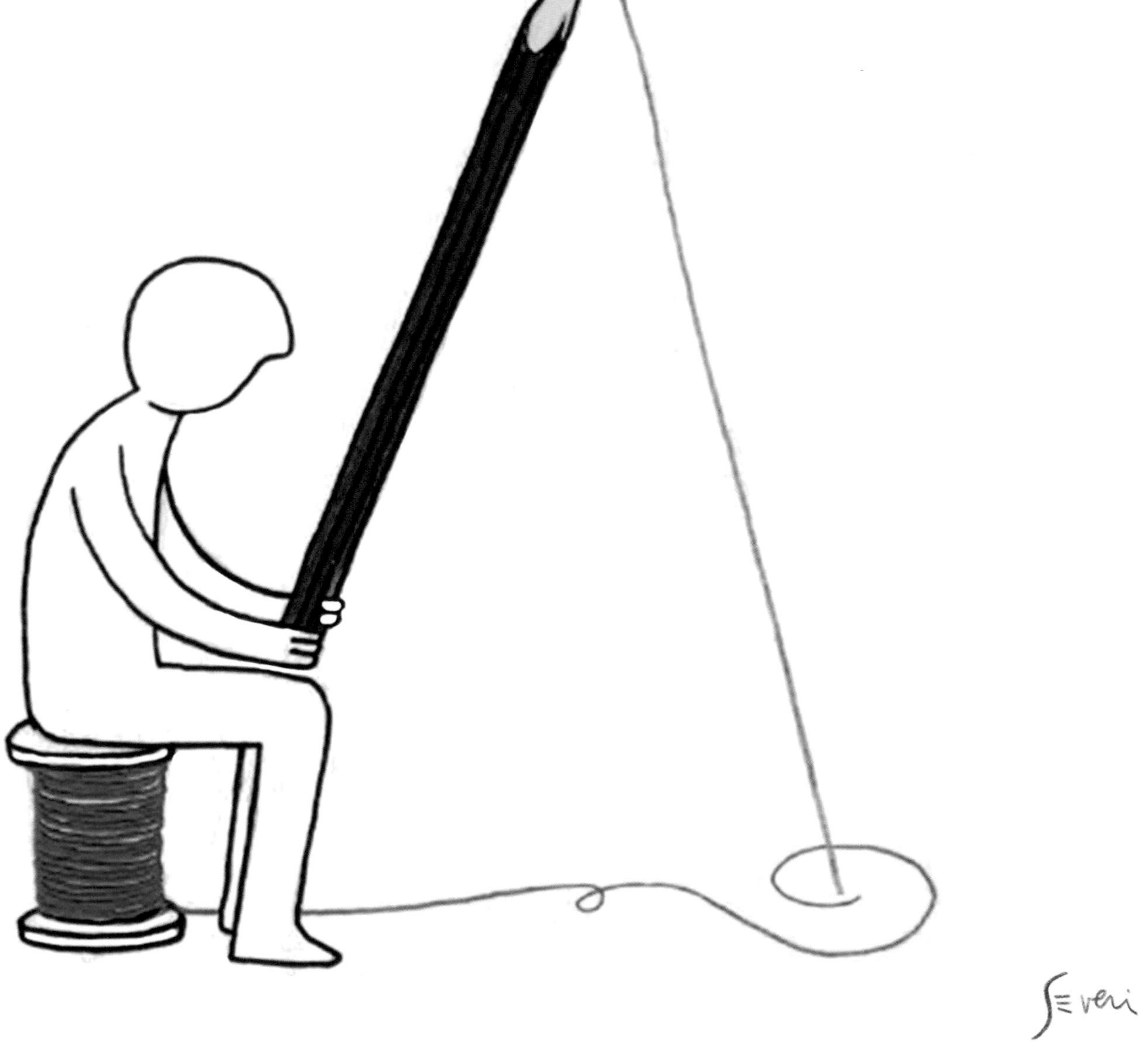
Severi

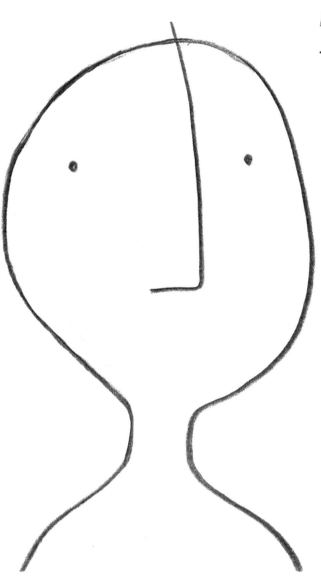

I HAVE SO MANY DOUBTS
ABOUT MY RELATIONSHIPS
THAT SOME TIMES I DOUBT
IF I AM THE RIGHT PERSON
TO BE WITH ME.

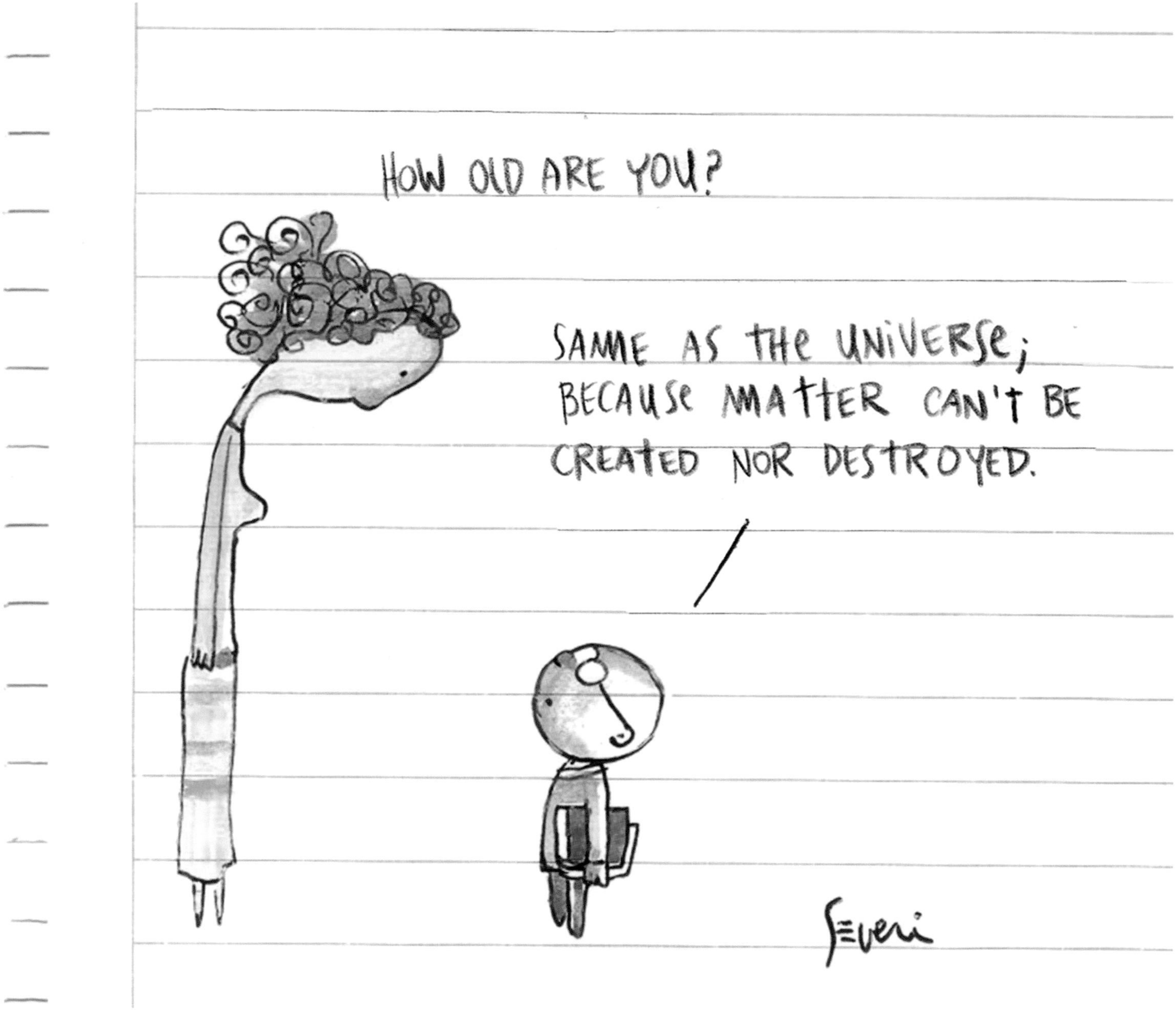
HOW OLD ARE YOU?
SAME AS THE UNIVERSE; BECAUSE MATTER CAN'T BE CREATED NOR DESTROYED.
Severi

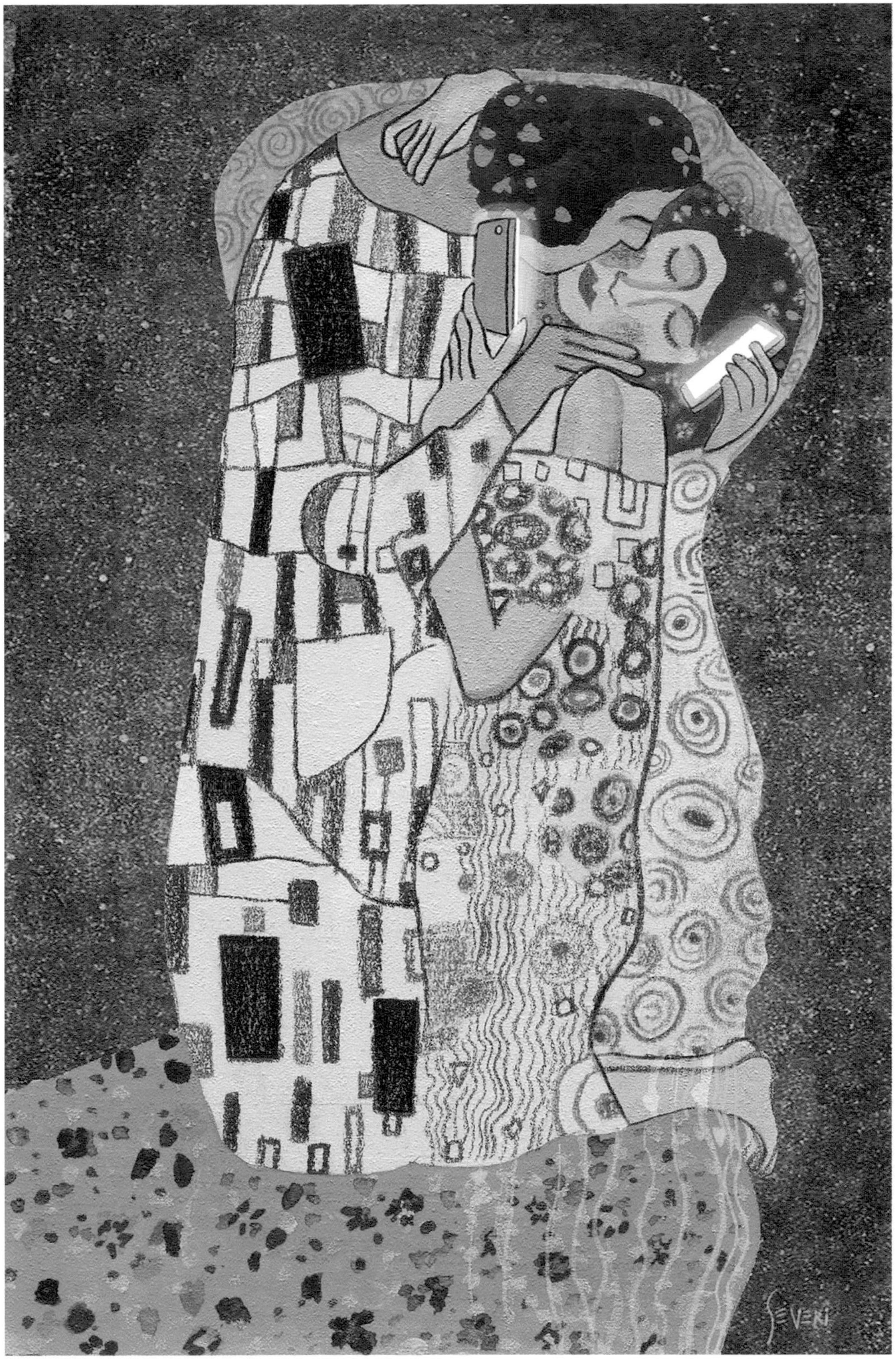

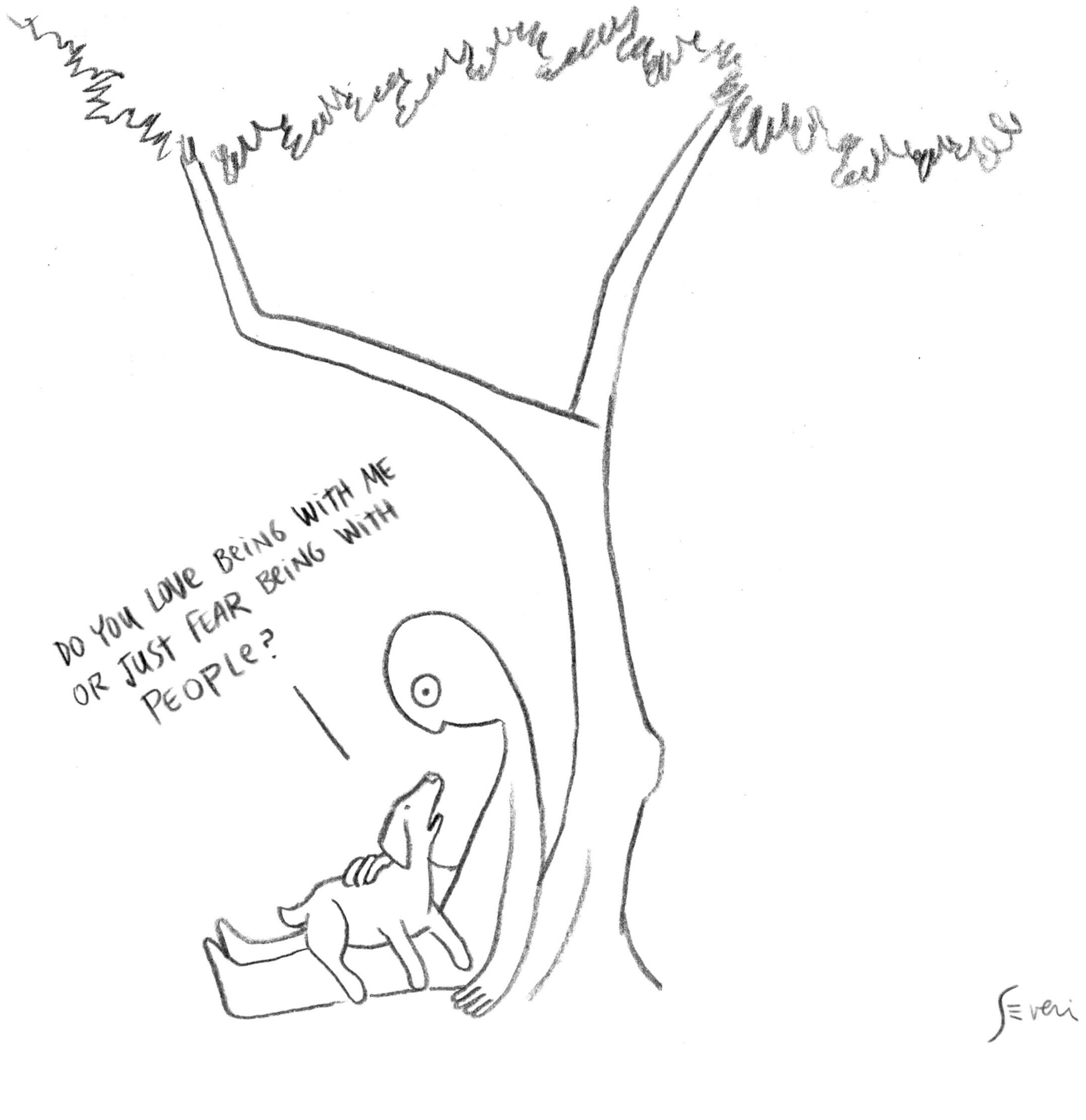
DO YOU LOVE BEING WITH ME
OR JUST FEAR BEING WITH
PEOPLE?
Severi

HOW NICE FINISHING
THE YEAR WITHOUT
GETTING BACK TOGETHER
WITH MY EX-SELF.

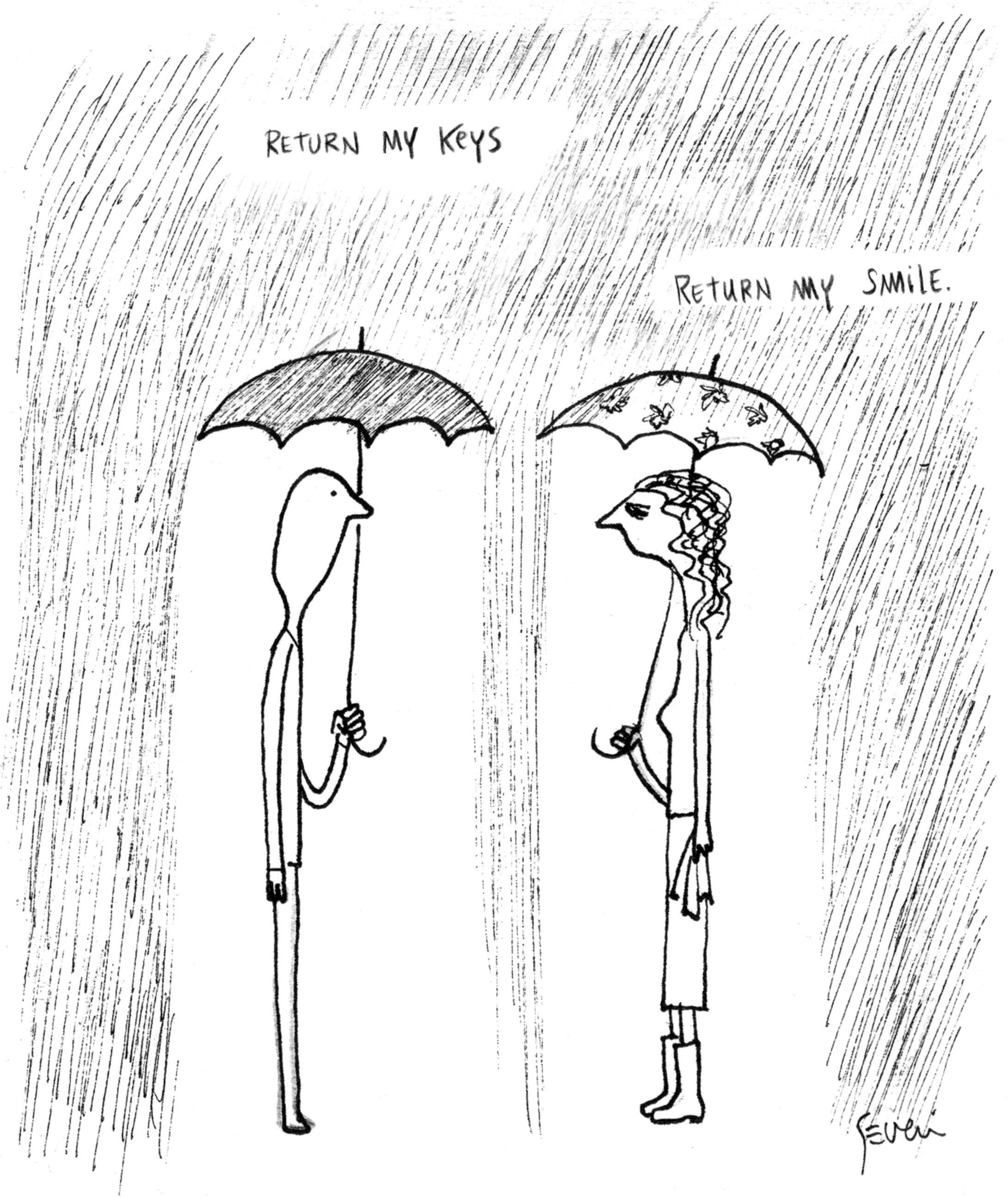

RETURN MY KEYS
RETURN MY SMILE.

IN THE END,
SIMPLE WINS.

Severi

THERE ARE HOMEY PEOPLE.

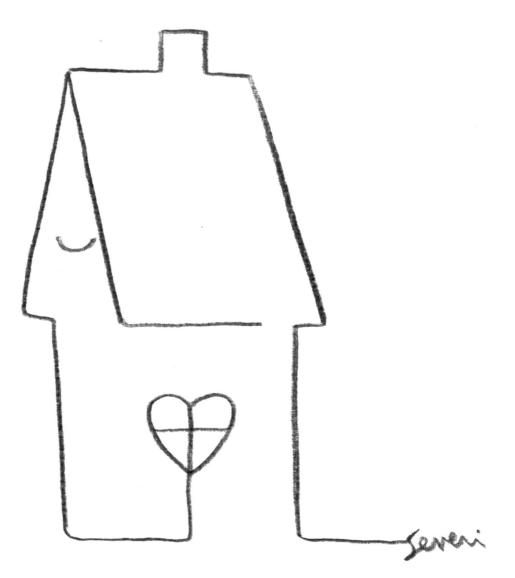

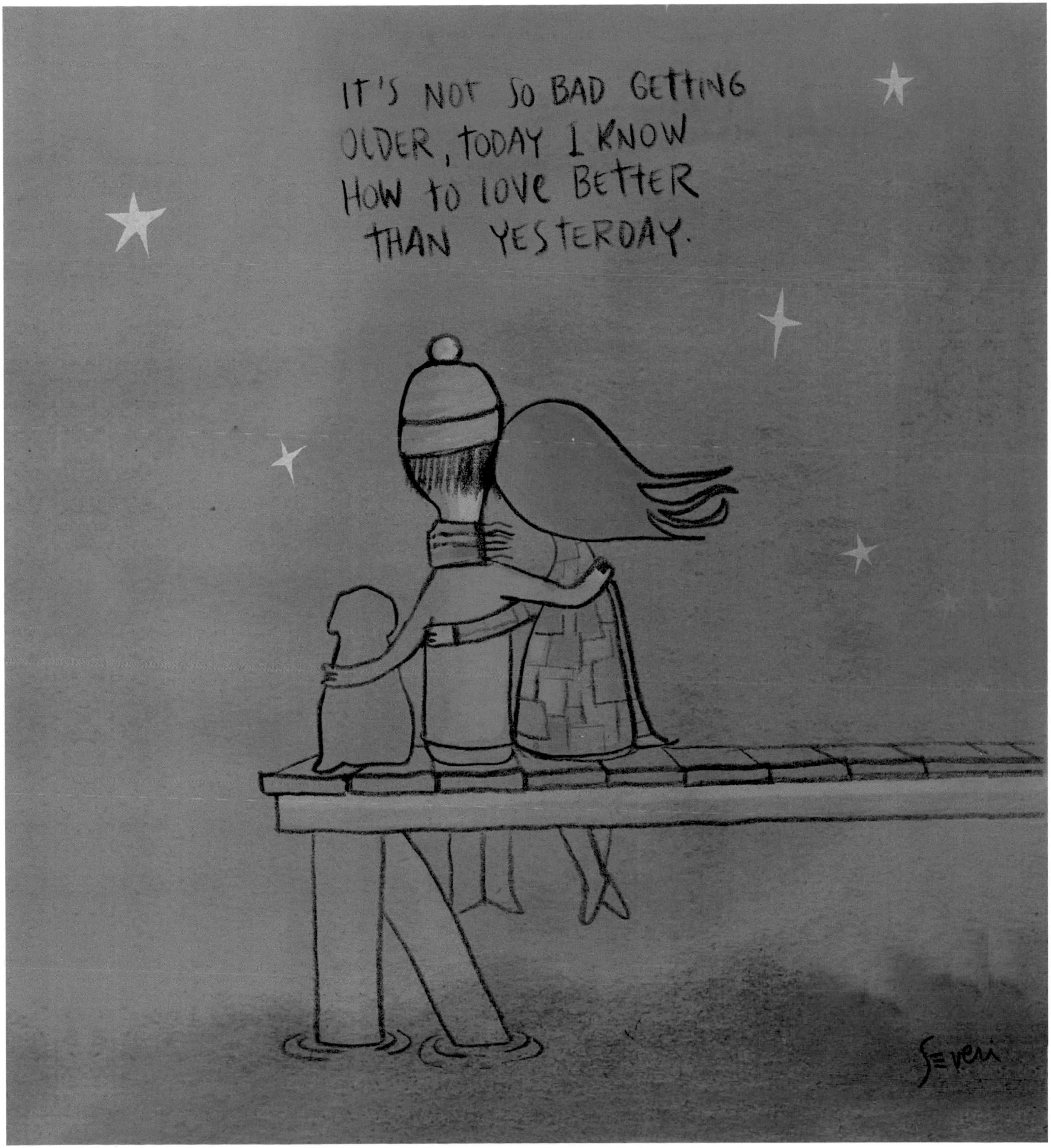
IT'S NOT SO BAD GETTING OLDER, TODAY I KNOW HOW TO LOVE BETTER THAN YESTERDAY.
Severi

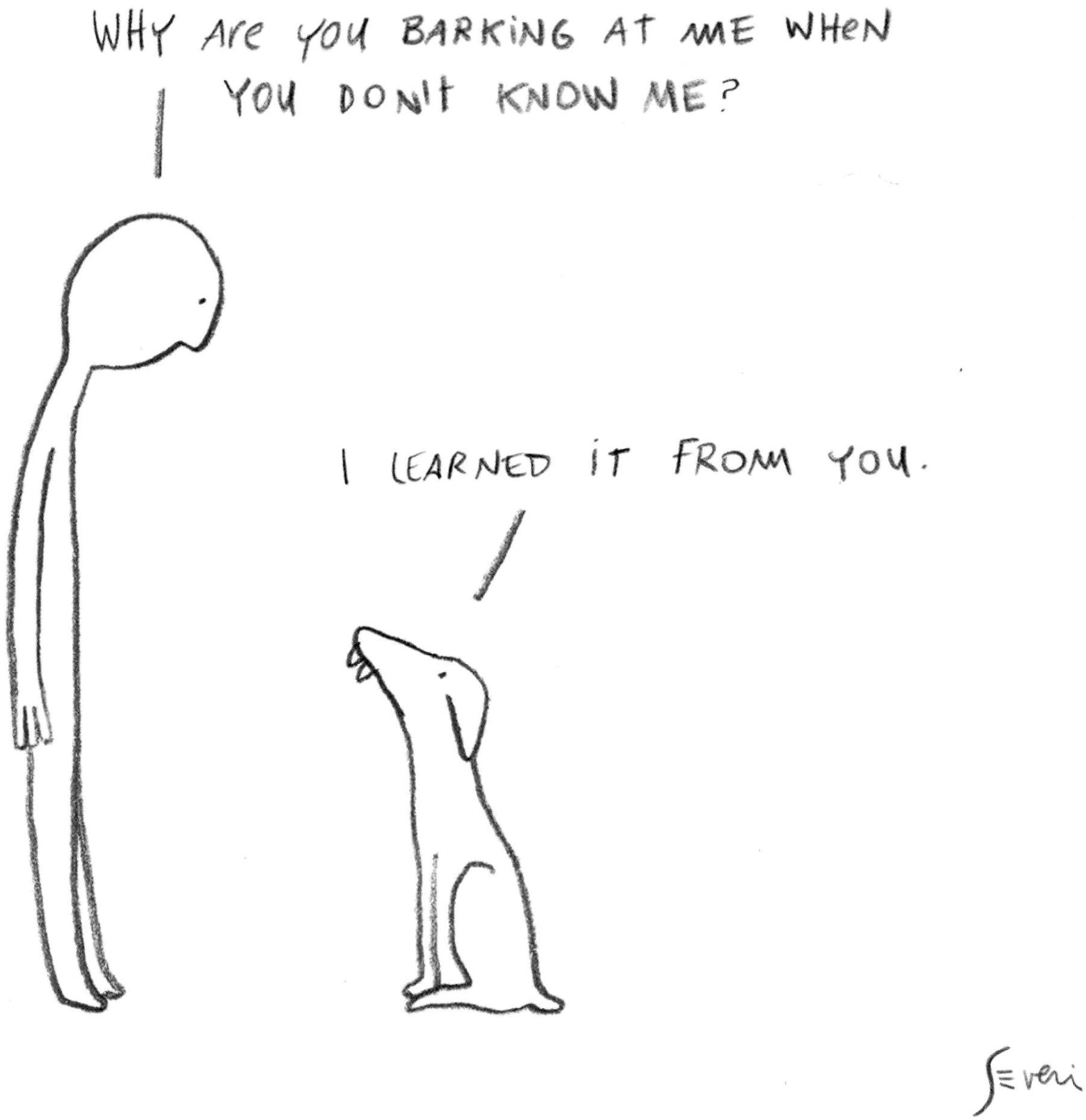
WHY ARE YOU BARKING AT ME WHEN YOU DON'T KNOW ME?
I LEARNED IT FROM YOU.
Severi

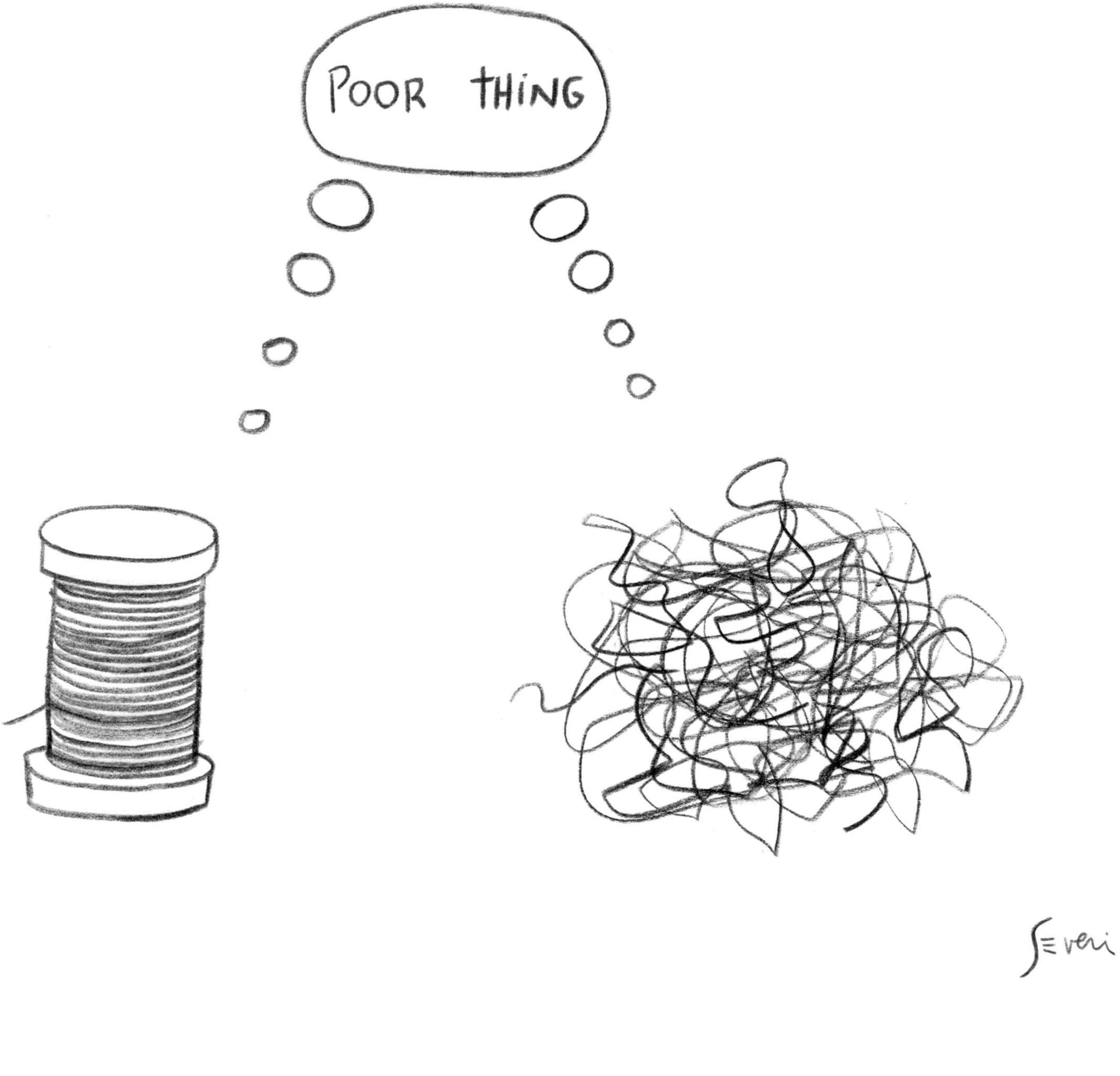
POOR THING
Severi

STRONG TIES HAVE NO KNOTS

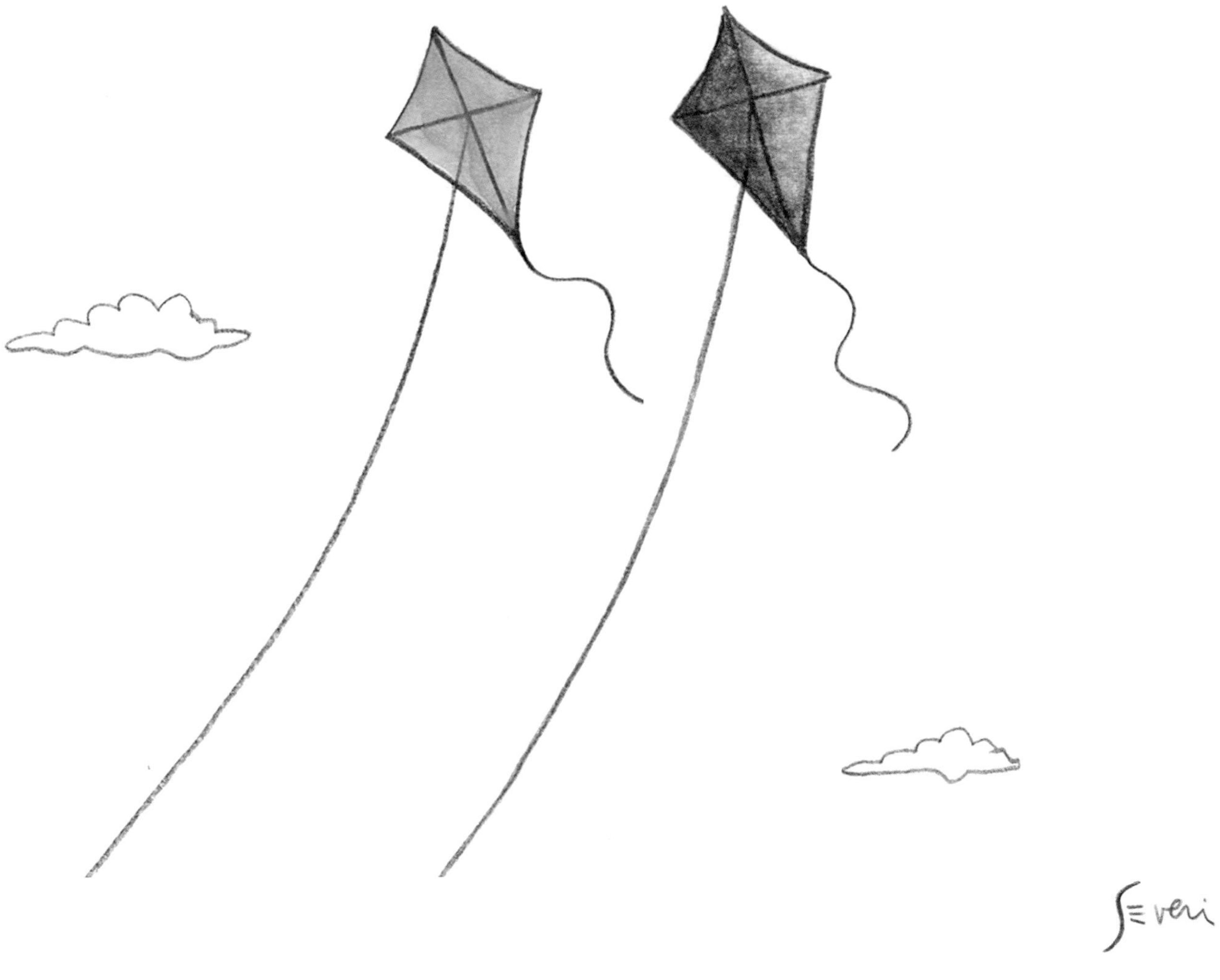
Severi

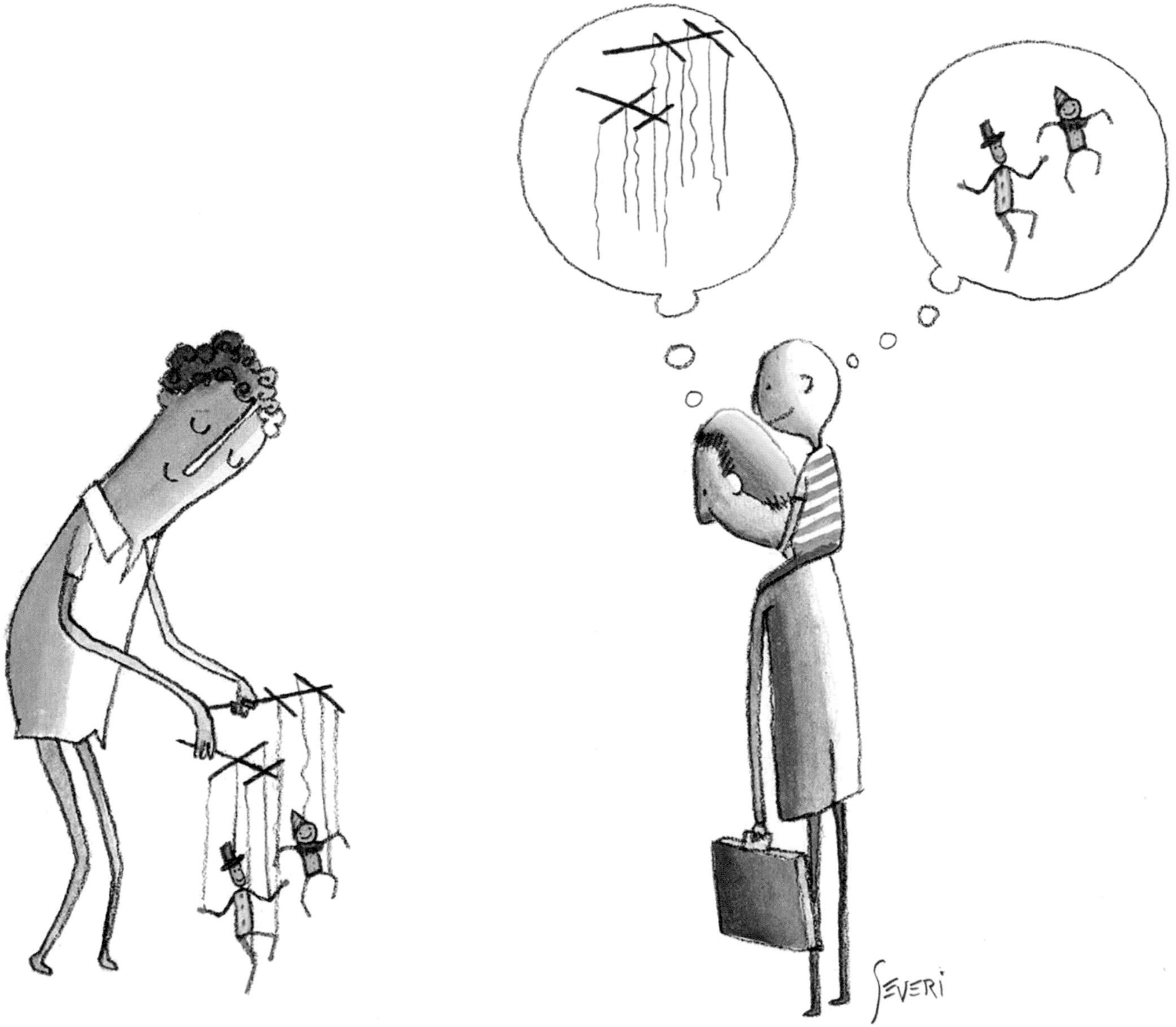
SEVERI

CURED BY THE HUG THAT DOES NOT JUDGE.

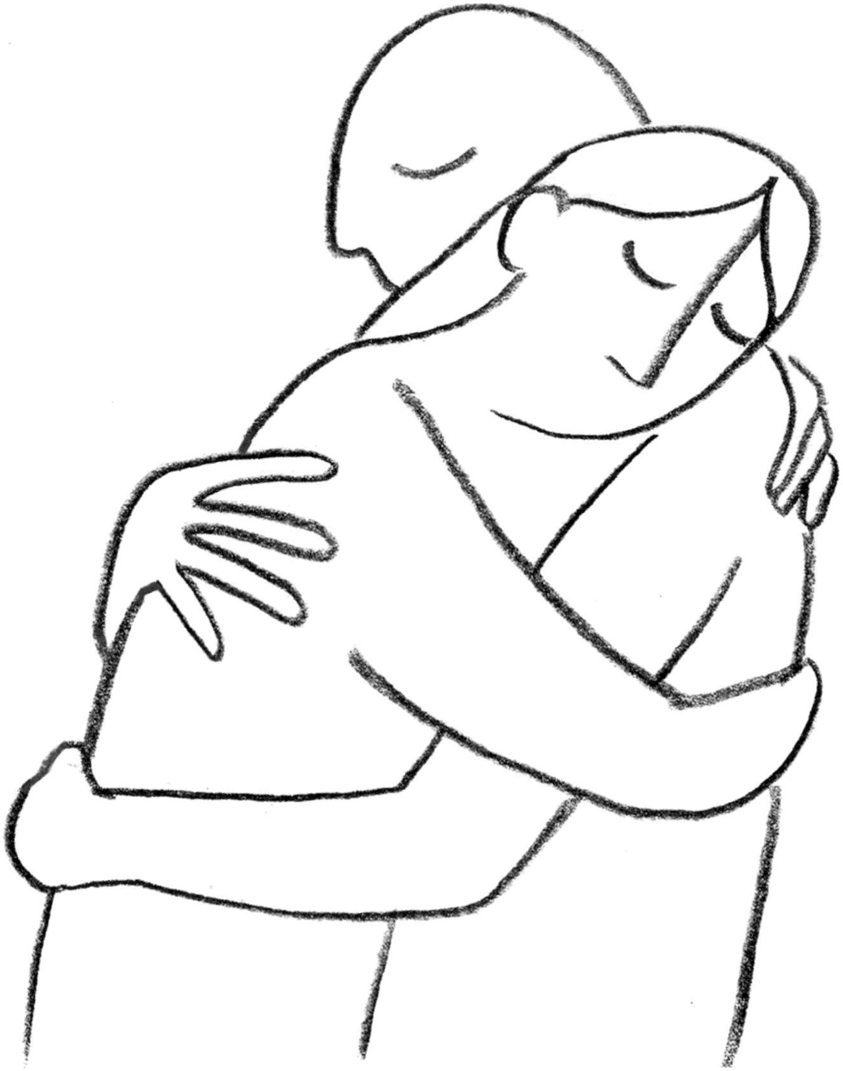

Severi

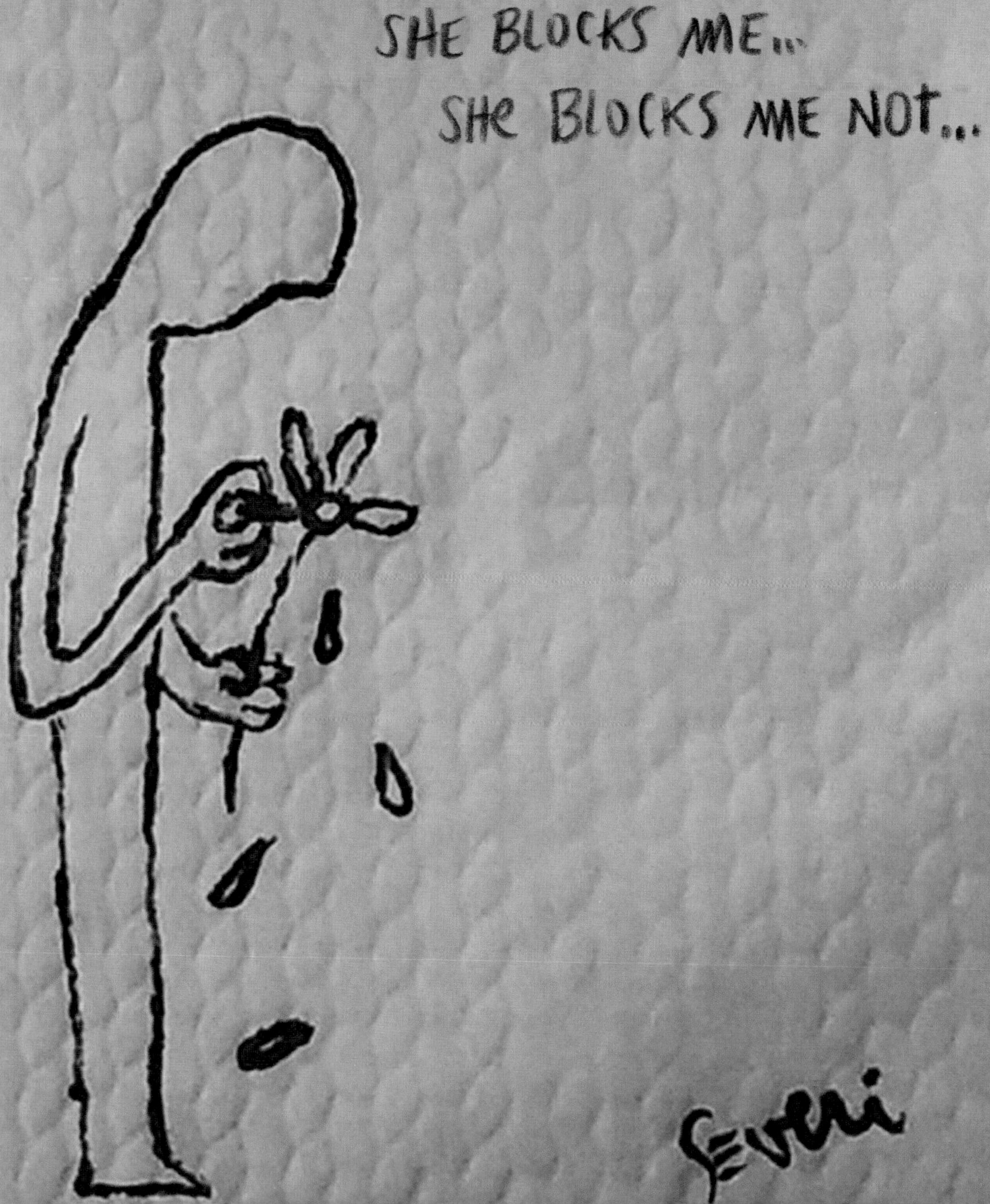
SHE BLOCKS ME...
SHE BLOCKS ME NOT...
Everi

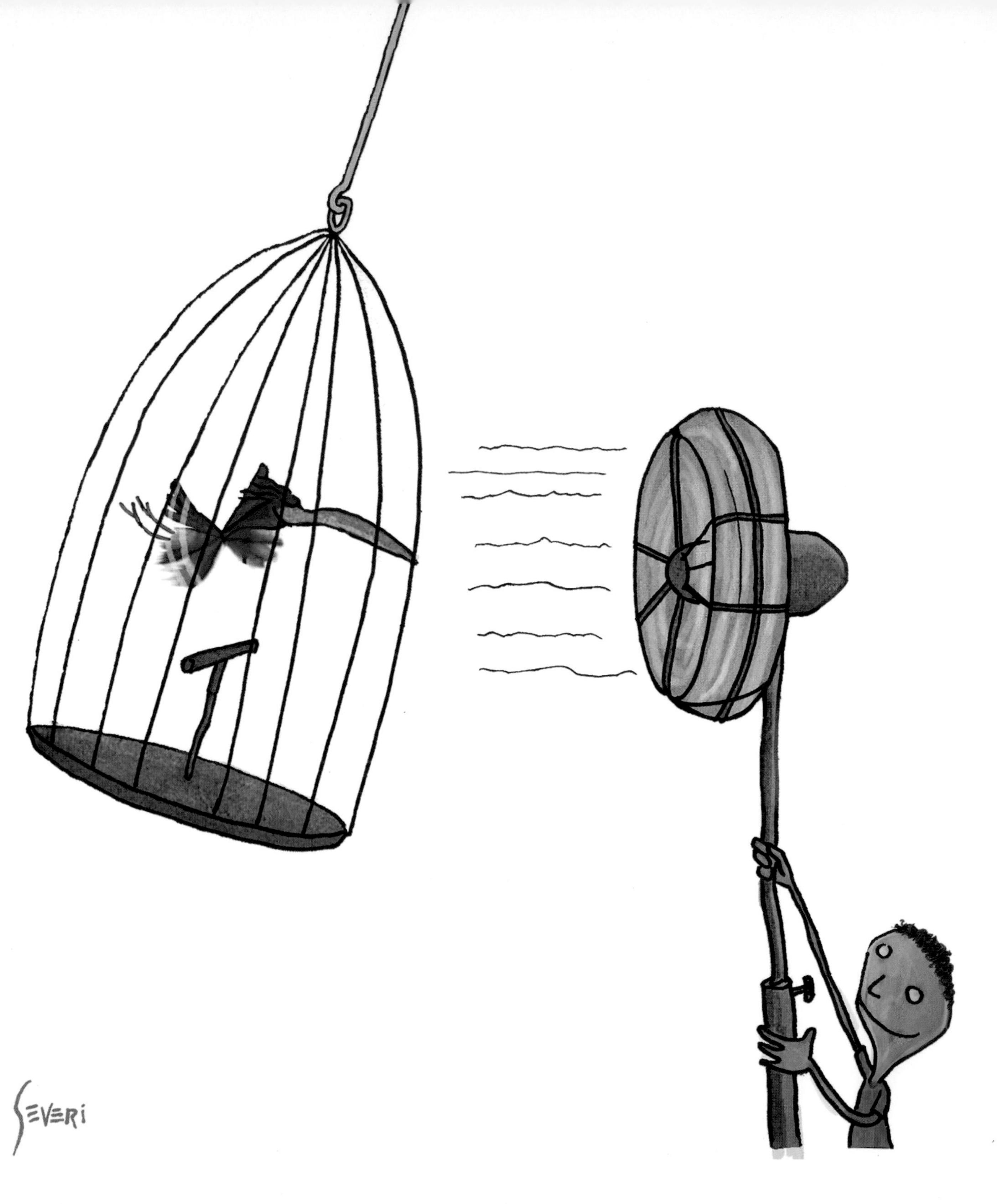
SEVERI

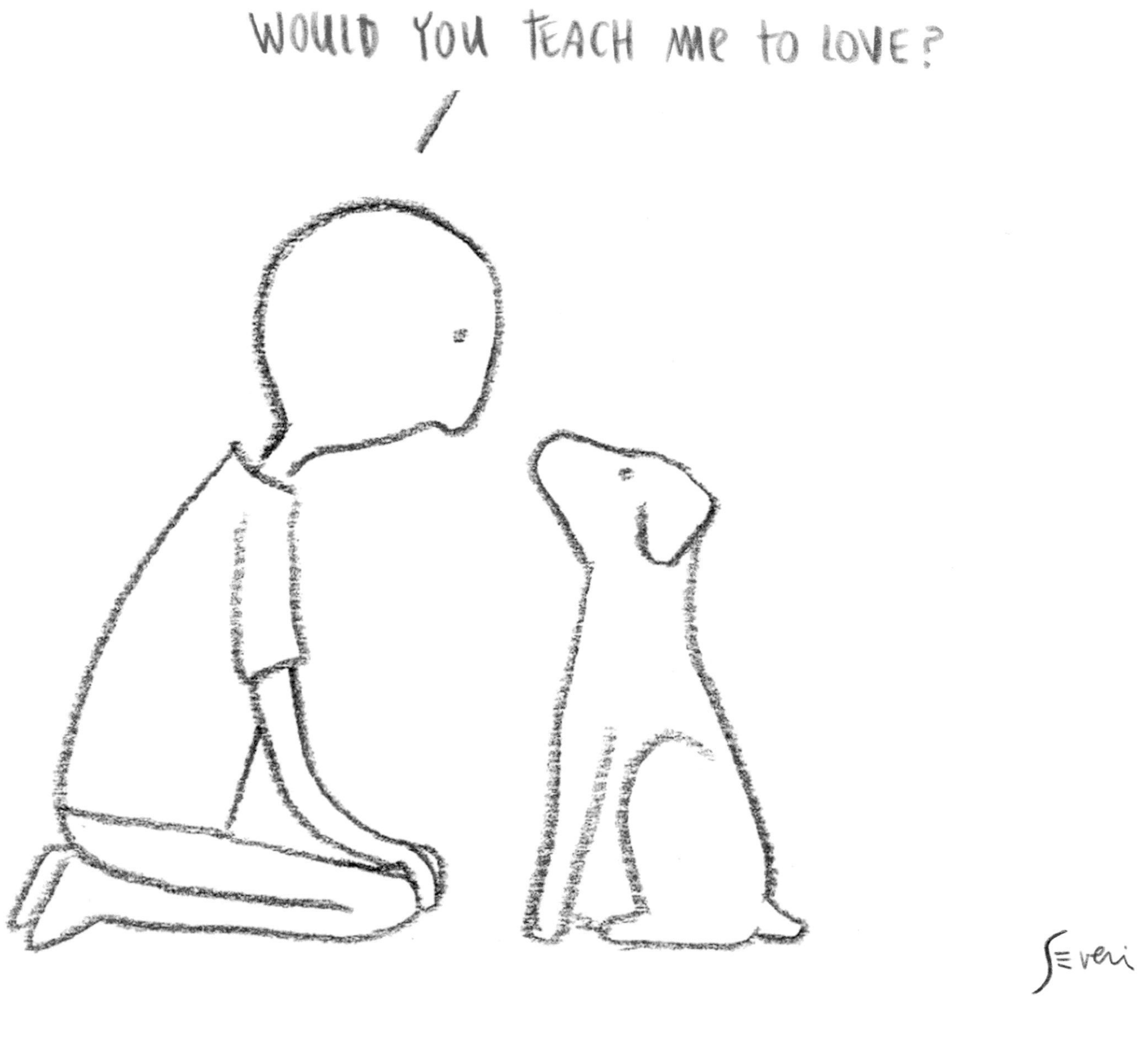
WOULD YOU TEACH ME TO LOVE?
Severi

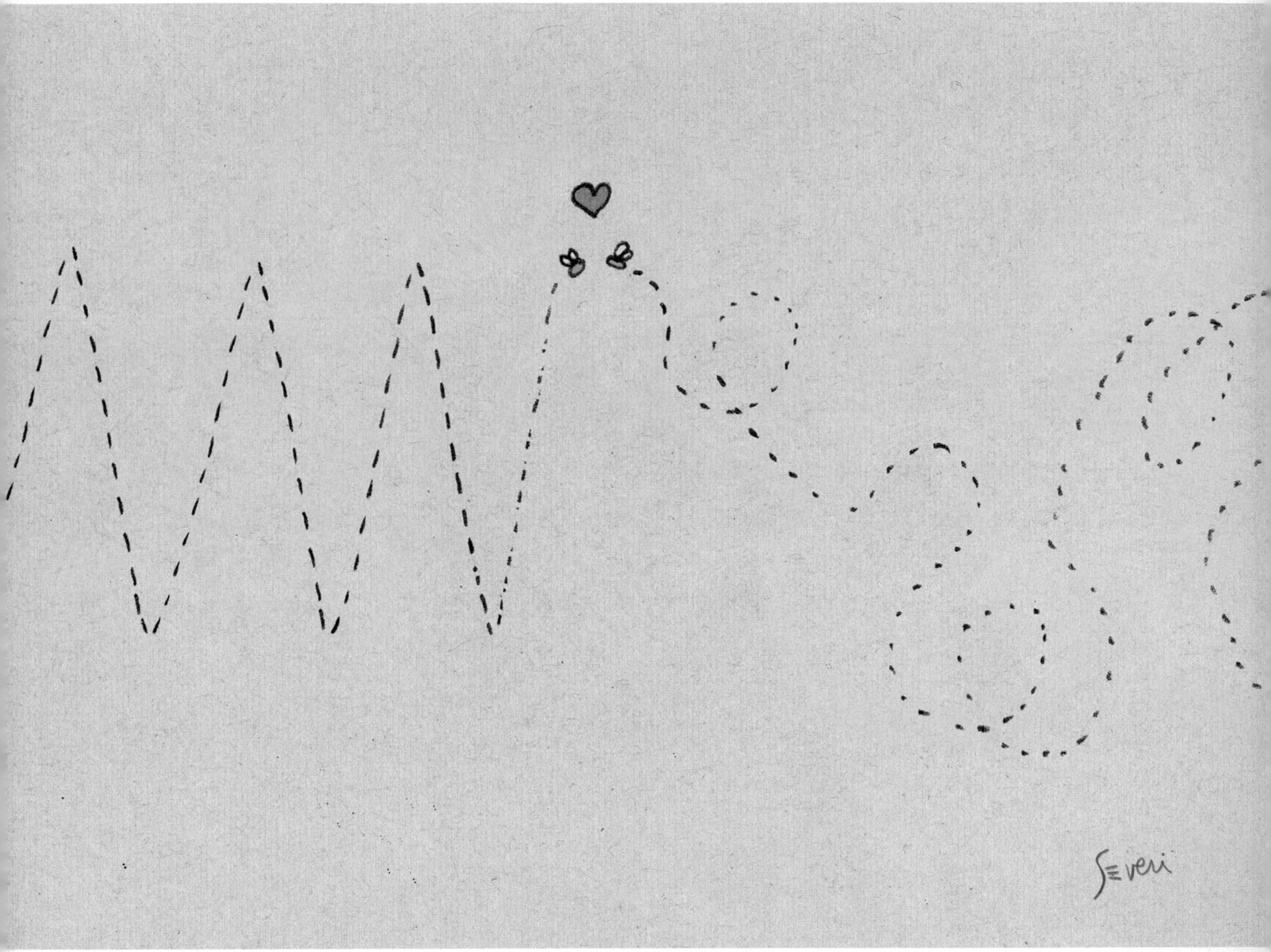
Severi

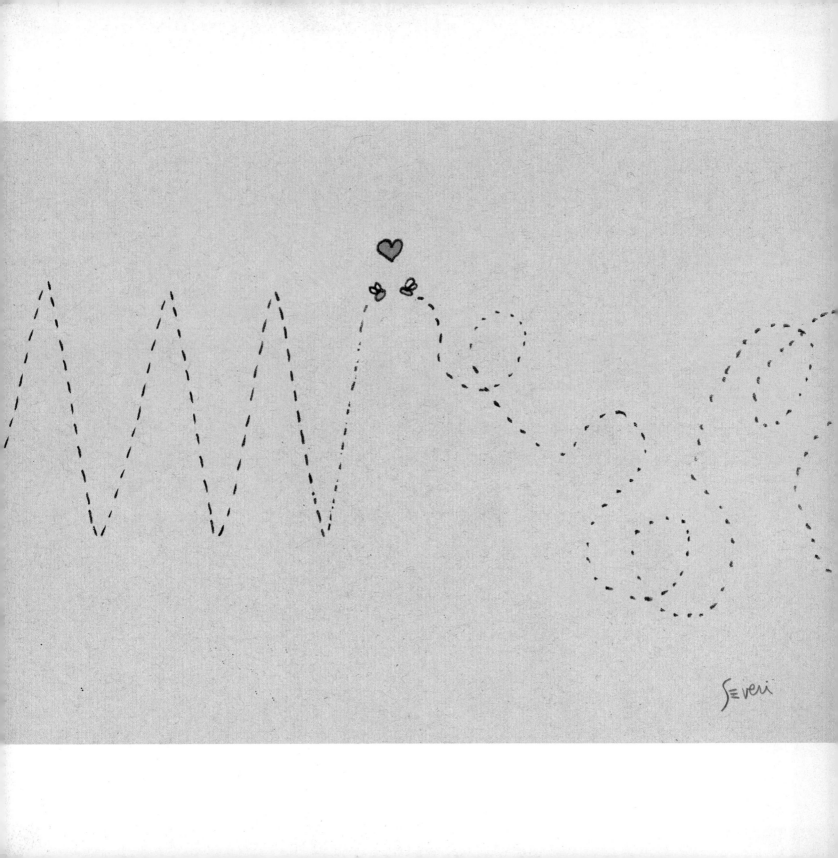

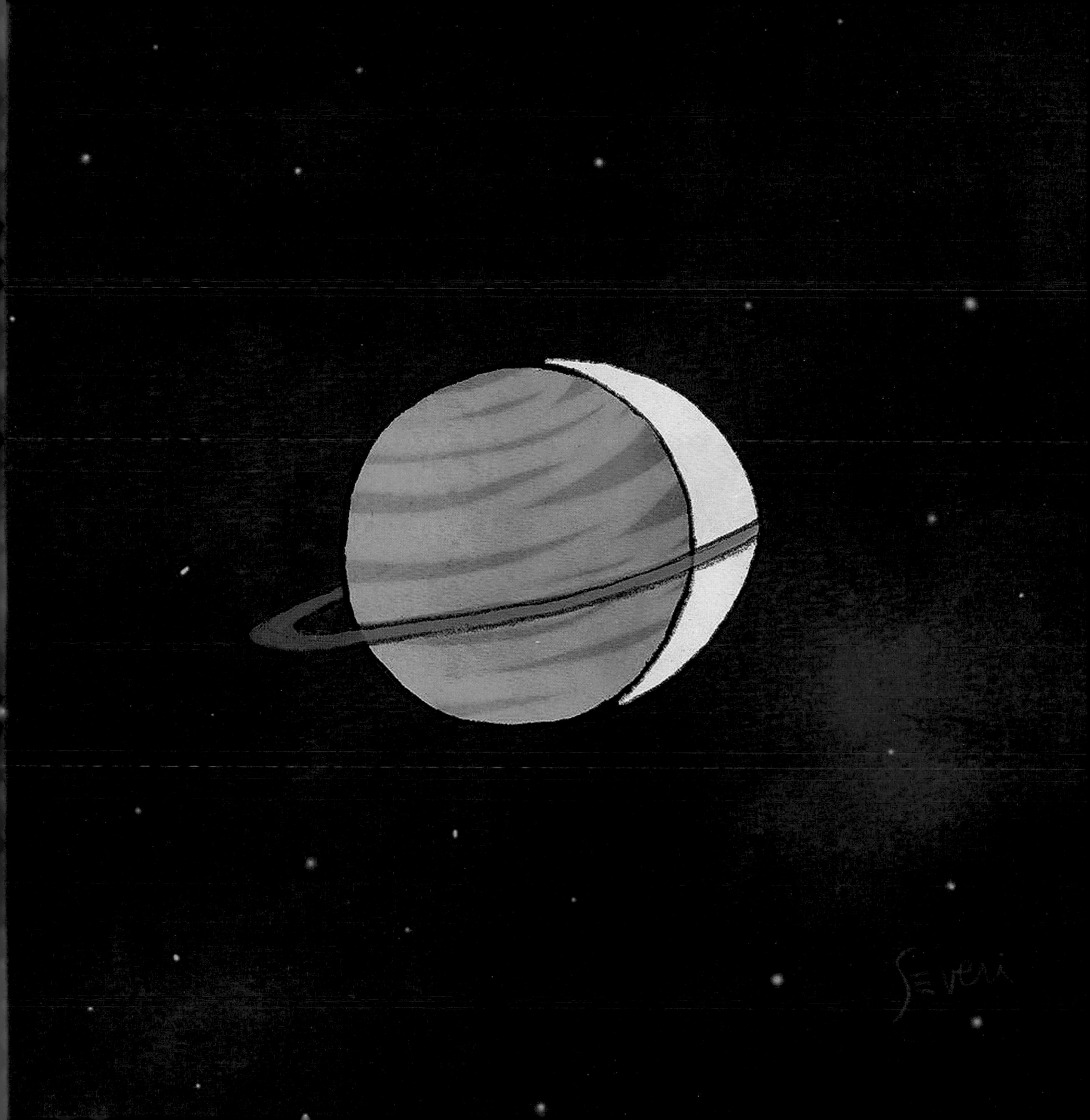

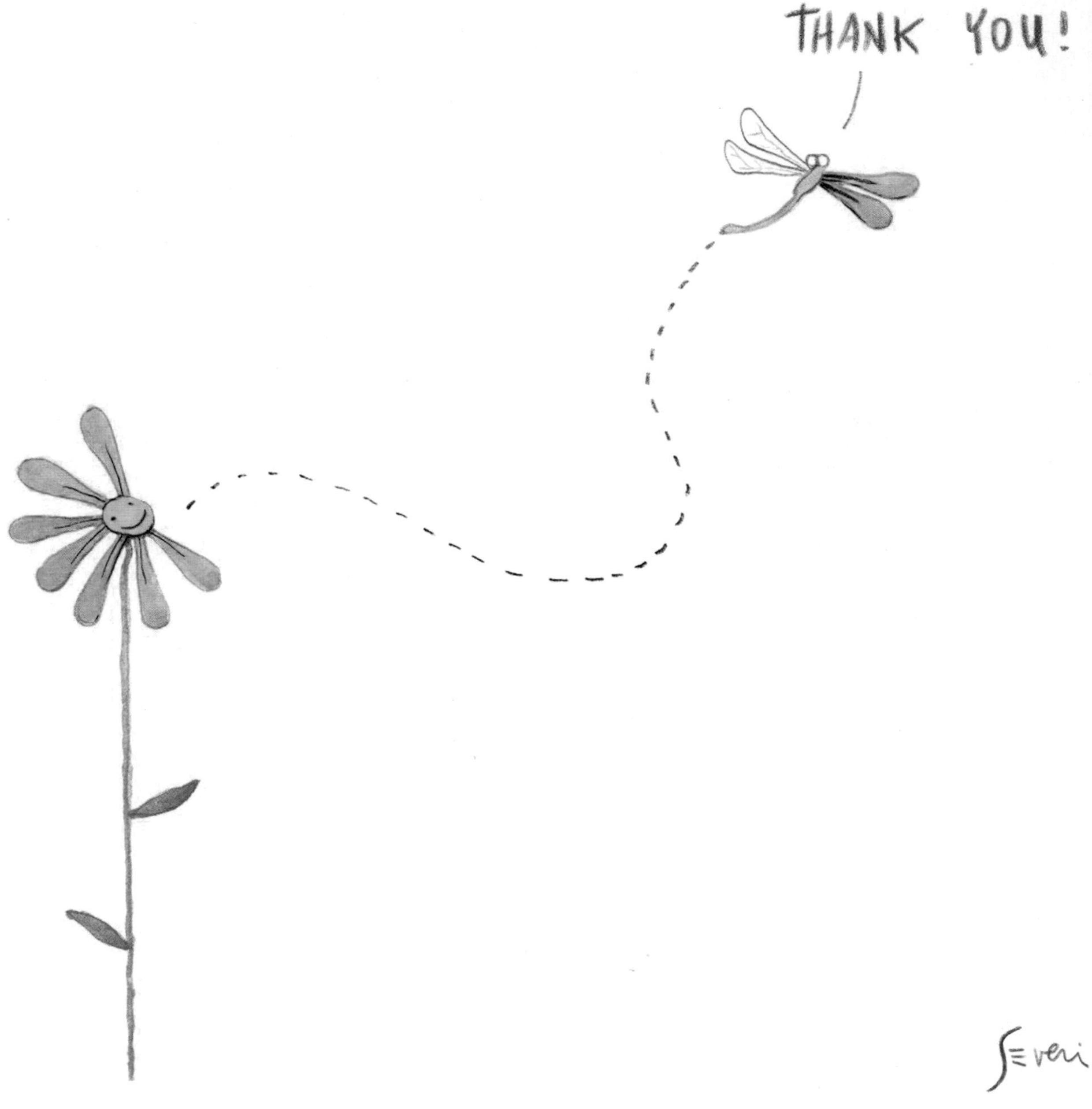
THANK YOU!
Severi

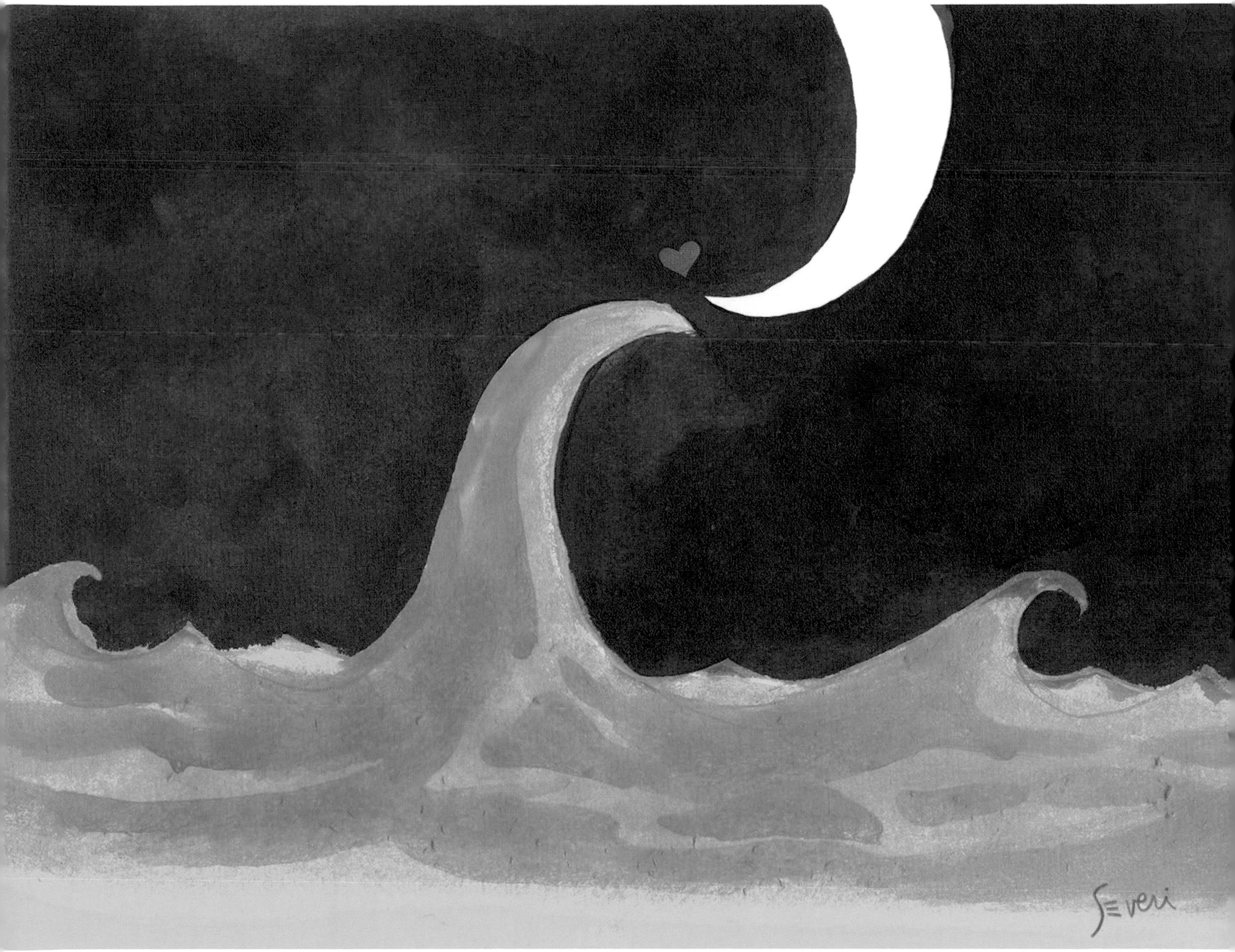
Severi

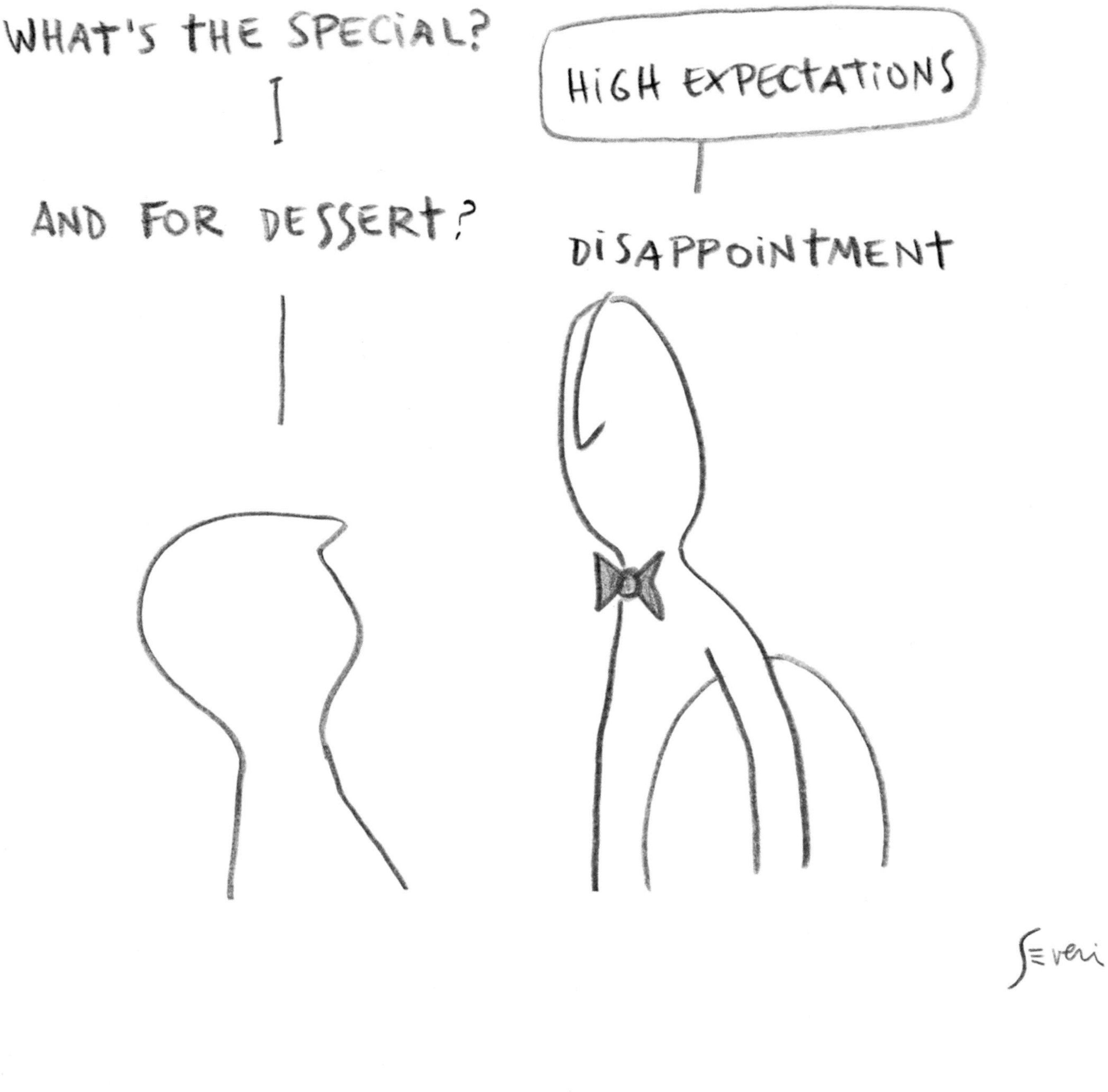
WHAT'S THE SPECIAL?
HIGH EXPECTATIONS
AND FOR DESSERT?
DISAPPOINTMENT
Severi

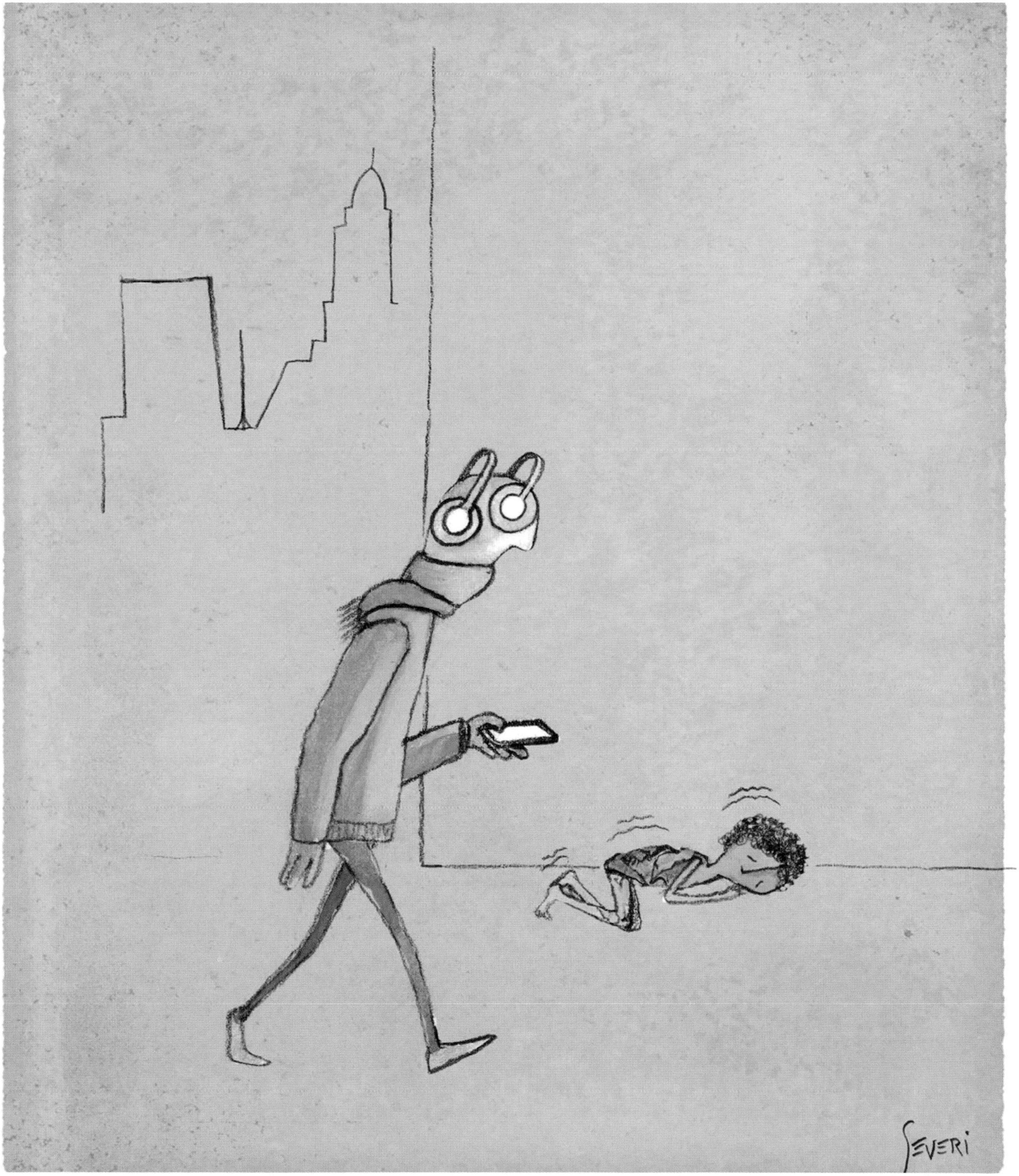
SEVERI

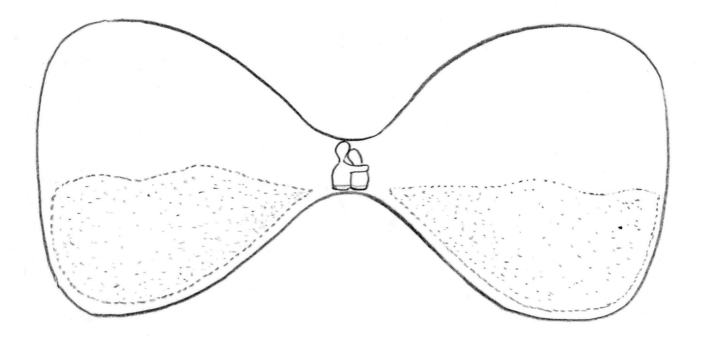

Severi

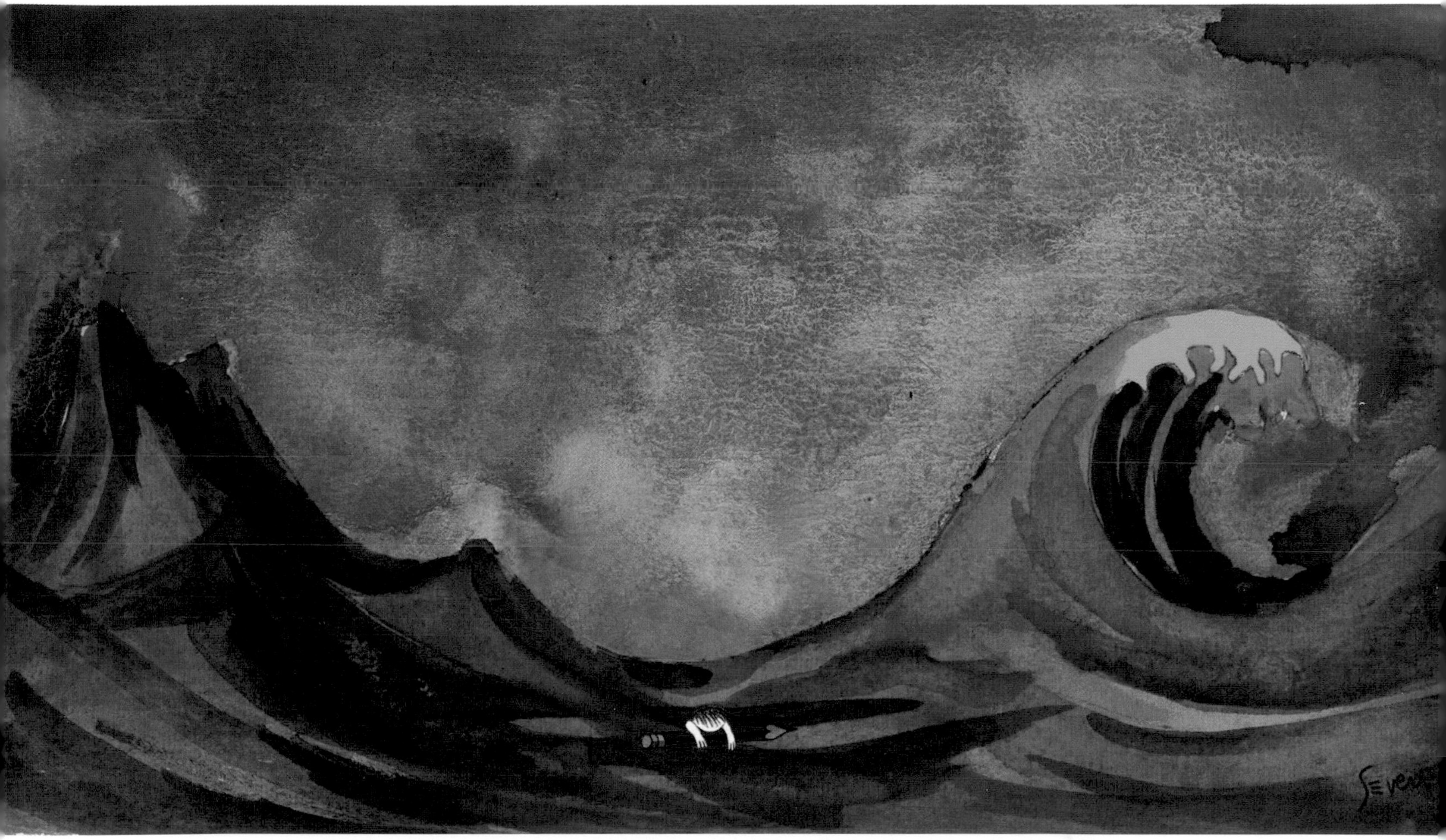

Acknowledgments

I am grateful for the support from all the readers that follow me on social media. Thank you for your baffling affection and respect for my work. All the energy that I receive from you morphs into fully-fledged projects and fuels dreams to come. Thank you to my family, for always being present. I feel your heart beat next to mine. Thank you as well to my other family, those friends that are my rock when I can't swim anymore, those homey people.

Thank you, Alejo, Enrique and your teams, for believing in this project. To my students, for their valuable suggestions, as well as to my many colleagues for their precious advice.

Thank you, Panchito, for your love and company.

Marcos Severi

Photo by Gaby leigue

MARCOS SEVERI

My name is Marcos and I love to draw. Like Forrest Gump said, I don't know much about anything. I was born in Buenos Aires, Argentina. My journey as an illustrator started when I was 17 years old. I published vignettes in some magazines and newspapers. One day I started a blog and began to publish whatever was on my mind. I never stopped. A blank page is my divan...

Recently I received my Art Degree. I live and work in the city of Buenos Aires with my cat Panchito.

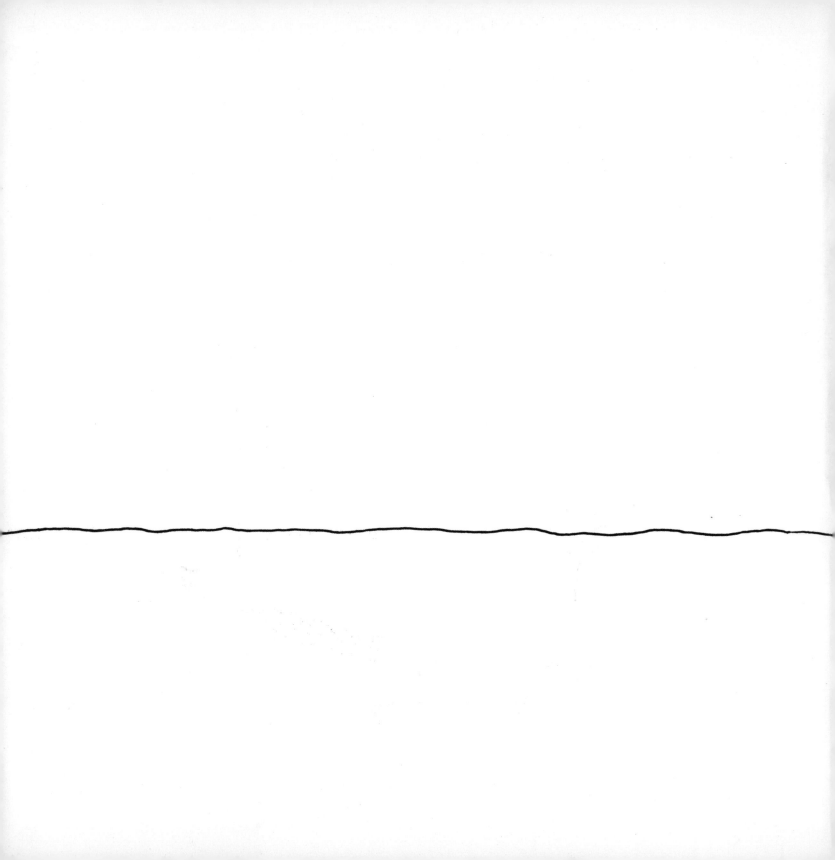